*the day before
happiness*

the day before
happiness

a novel

erri de luca

translated by Michael F. Moore

OTHER PRESS
New York

Copyright © 2009 Giangiacomo Feltrinelli Editore Milano

Originally published in Italian as *Il giorno prima della felicità*
by Giangiacomo Feltrinelli Editore, Mailan, in 2009, by
arrangement with Susanna Zevi Agenzia Letteraria.

Translation copyright © 2011 Michael F. Moore

Production Editor: *Yvonne E. Cárdenas*
Text Designer: *Simon M. Sullivan*
This book was set in 12 pt Janson by Alpha Design &
Composition of Pittsfield, NH.

10 9 8 7 6 5 4 3 2 1

LIBRARY OF CONGRESS CATALOGING-IN-PUBLICATION DATA

De Luca, Erri, 1950–
  [Giorno prima della felicità. English]
  The day before happiness / by Erri De Luca ; translated by
Michael F. Moore.
      p. cm.
  ISBN 978-1-59051-481-8 (hardcover : acid-free paper) — ISBN
978-1-59051-482-5 (ebook) 1. Naples (Italy)—History—1945—
Fiction. I. Moore, Michael, 1954 Aug. 24– II. Title.

  PQ4864.E5498G5613 2011
  853'.914—dc23

                            2011030641

Much of this novel takes place in a small office-apartment known as the *portineria*, which I have translated here as the doorman's loge. Generally located in the entryway of an apartment complex, the loge may have one or two rooms: a front room with a door, a picture window, a table and a small stove, and perhaps a small room in the back. The sleeping quarters are located in another part of the complex. A uniquely Neapolitan dwelling that figures in the novel is the *basso*, a one- or two-room ground-floor apartment opening directly onto the street in the oldest and poorest neighborhoods. The primary building material of the city is the soft volcanic rock known as *tufo*. Dug into the tufo substratum of Naples is an underground city of tunnel networks, spacious cavities, cisterns, and even the remains of the ancient Greek and Roman city, Neapolis.

In Neapolitan dialect it is common to truncate words and names, so the doorman, Don Gaetano, becomes *Gaeta'* (pronounced "guy-tah"), while the unnamed narrator, the *guaglione* (gwhile-yoh-ne)—a generic name for a boy or young man—is shortened to *guaglio*. The vowels tend to be more open than in standard Italian while the consonants are often doubled.

The card game that Don Gaetano and the guaglione play is *scopa*, literally "sweep," since the object is to take all forty cards and thus do a sweep. While it is played throughout Italy, the deck design and nomenclature can vary by city or region. The four suits of the Neapolitan deck are: *spade* (swords), *coppe* (cups), *bastoni* (clubs), and *denari* (coins). There are two ways to take a trick: by playing a single card to take a card of equal value, called a *pariglio* since an even number of cards of the same value will remain in the deck; or by playing a single card to take two or more cards whose sum adds up to the same value, called a *spariglio* since an odd number of cards of the same value will remain in the deck.

The history the narrator learns in school is of the Risorgimento, the process of Italian unification that was secured through three wars of independence: in 1848, 1859–1861, and 1866–1970. There was a strong rift within the movement between proponents of a republic, most famously General Giuseppe Garibaldi and Giuseppe Mazzini; and the monarchists, particularly

Count Cavour, the first prime minister. Carlo Pisacane was an early anarchist. Two historic battles were fought with the Austrians at Custoza, near Verona: in 1848, during the First War of Independence, and in 1866, during the Third War of Independence.

The war stories told by Don Gaetano are based on the Four Days of Naples, the popular uprising of September 27–30, 1943. As the Allied forces closed in on the city, the Nazi occupiers laid plans to blow up the harbor, round up able-bodied men and youths, and deport them to labor camps. When the Germans began summary executions of the men who did not show up for deportation, the Resistance and the populace fought them with and without regular weapons through acts of sabotage, guerrilla warfare, and open battle.

the day before
happiness

i discovered the hiding place when the soccer ball ended up there. Behind the statue's niche, in the courtyard of the building, was a trapdoor covered by two wooden boards. I noticed they were moving when I stood on them. I got scared, recovered the ball, and wriggled out between the statue's legs.

Only a skinny child contortionist like myself could slip his head and body between the slightly parted legs of the warrior king, after twisting past the sword planted right before his feet. The ball had gotten stuck in there after ricocheting between the sword and the leg.

I pushed it through, and while I was squirming to get out, the others returned to the game. Traps are easy to get into but getting out takes some sweat. To make matters worse, fear was making me rush. I went back to my place in the goal. They let me play with them because I got the ball back no matter where it ended up. A customary destination was the balcony on the first floor, an abandoned apartment. Rumor had it a ghost lived there. Old buildings had trapdoors in the walls, secret passageways, crime and love stories. Old buildings were dens of ghosts.

. . .

This is how it went the first time I climbed up to the terrace. From the little window on the ground floor of the courtyard where I lived, I was watching the bigger boys play one afternoon. The ball shot up in the air off a bad kick and ended up on the second-floor terrace. A vinyl ball slightly deflated from use, it was lost. While they were arguing over the quandary, I stuck my head out and asked if they would let me play with them. Yes, if you buy us another ball. No, with that one, I replied. Their curiosity aroused, they accepted. I grabbed hold of a rain pipe, a downspout, which passed next to the terrace and continued up to the roof. It was small and attached to the courtyard wall with rusty clamps. I started to climb, the pipe was covered with dust, the grip was less sure than I had imagined. But I had made a promise. I looked up: behind the glass of a third-floor window there she was, the little girl I was trying to get a peek of. She was in her spot, head resting on her hands. Usually she was looking up at the sky. Not this time. She was looking down.

. . .

I had to keep going and I did. Sixteen feet is a big drop for a child. I climbed up the pipe, bracing my feet on the clamps until I was at the same height as the terrace. Below me the comments had quieted down. I extended my left hand to grab on to the iron railing, I was short by a palm. So I had to trust my feet and reach over with the hand holding on to the rain pipe. I decided to do it in a single swoop, and I reached it with my left. Now I had to bring over my right. I tightened my grip on the iron railing and flung out my right hand to grab hold. I lost my footing: for a moment my hands held my body suspended in thin air, then up swung a knee, then two feet, and I climbed over. How come I wasn't afraid? I realized my fear is shy, it needs to be alone to come out into the open. But the eyes of the other boys were below and hers were above. My fear was embarrassed to come out. It would get even with me later, that night in bed in the dark, with the rustling of ghosts in thin air.

. . .

I threw the ball down, they went back to playing, ignoring me. The descent was easier, I could stretch my hand out toward the rain pipe counting on two solid supports for my feet on the balcony's edge. Before lunging for the pipe I took a quick glance at the third floor. I had volunteered for the task hoping she would notice me, the little dust brush from the courtyard. There she was, eyes open wide. Before I could attempt a smile she had disappeared. Stupid to look and see whether she was looking. You were supposed to believe without second-guessing, as you do with guardian angels. I got mad at myself, sliding down the pipe to get off the stage. The prize, admission to the game, was waiting for me below. They placed me in the goal and so was my role decided. I was goalie.

. . .

From that day on they called me *'a scigna*, the monkey. I would dive between their feet to grab the ball and save the goal. The goalie is the last defense, the hero in the trenches. I got kicked in the hands, in the face, I didn't cry. I was proud to play with the bigger boys, who were nine even ten years old.

The ball ended up on the balcony other times, I would get to it in less than a minute. In front of the goal I defended was a puddle from a leak. At first it would be clear, I could see the girl in the window by reflection while my team was attacking. I didn't run into her, I didn't know what the rest of her body was like under that face resting on her hands. On sunny days I could find my way to her through the ricocheting of her reflection. I would keep staring at her until my eyes welled up with tears from the light. The closed glass of the courtyard windows allowed the reflection containing her to travel all the way down to my shadowy corner. So many rounds of her portrait to reach my little window. A television set had recently arrived at an apartment in the building, I heard you could see people and animals moving on it, without color. But I could watch the little girl with the rich brown of her hair, the green of her dress, the yellow added by the sun.

· · ·

I went to school. My foster mother enrolled me, but I never saw her. Don Gaetano, the doorman, took care of me. He brought me a hot meal in the evening. In the morning before school I would bring him back the clean plate and he would warm me a cup of milk. I lived alone in the little room. Don Gaetano spoke very little, he too had grown up an orphan, but in an orphanage, not like me, running free in a building and going out into the city.

I liked school, the teacher spoke to the children. I came from the little room where no one spoke to me, and at school there was someone you had to listen to. It was nice to have a man who explained to the children the numbers, the years of history, the places of geography. There was a colored map of the world, someone who had never left the city could find out about Africa, which was green, the South Pole, white, Australia, yellow, and the oceans, blue. The continents and islands were in the feminine gender, the seas and mountains masculine.

At school there were the poor kids and the others. The poverty cases like me would get a slice of bread with quince jam, brought in by the janitor. A fresh baked smell came in with him that made our mouths water. Nothing for the others, they already had a snack brought from home. Another difference was that the poverty cases had their heads shaved in spring for lice, the others kept their hair.

We used to write with a fountain pen and ink was available at every desk inside a hole. To write was to paint: you dipped the pen in, let the drops fall until one remained, and with that you managed to write half a word. Then you dipped again. We poverty cases would dry the sheet of paper with our warm breath. Below our breath, the blue of the ink trembled while it changed color. The other children dried with blotting paper. Our gesture was more beautiful, blowing wind over the flattened paper. The others instead crushed their words beneath a white card.

. . .

In the courtyard the children played amid the past remote of the centuries. The city was ancient, excavated, filled with grottoes and hiding places. In the summer afternoons when the tenants went on vacation or disappeared behind the blinds, I used to go to a second courtyard where the opening of a well was covered by wooden boards. I would sit on top of them, listening. From below, who knows how deep, came a rustling of moving water. Locked up down there was a life, a prisoner, an ogre, a fish. Cool air rose up between the boards and dried my sweat. In childhood I had the most precious freedom. Children are explorers. They want to learn secrets.

So I went back behind the statue to see where the trapdoor led. It was August, the month when children grow the fastest.

One early afternoon I squeezed between the feet and the sword of the statue, a copy of the King Ruggero the Norman in front of the Palazzo Reale. The wooden boards were fastened tight, they moved but couldn't be lifted. I had brought my spoon with me, I used it to pry at the encrustations. I placed the two boards off to the side, below was the darkness, descending. Fear rushed in, taking advantage of the fact that no one was around. You couldn't hear the sound of water, it was a dry darkness. After a while fear grows tired. Even the darkness became less compact, I could see a couple of rungs of a wooden ladder descending. I reached out my arm to touch the support, it was solid, dusty. I covered the passage back up with the boards, I had discovered enough for one day.

· · ·

I went back with a candle. A coolness rose from the darkness and grazed my short-panted legs. I descended into a grotto. Underneath the city is the void on which it rests. Our solid mass above is matched by an equal amount of shadow below, bearing the body of the city.

When I touched the ground I lit the candle. It was the cigarette smugglers' depot. I knew they went for offshore pickups in motorboats. I had discovered a storeroom. Having hoped for a treasure, I was disappointed. There had to be another entrance, those boxes couldn't fit between the legs of the king. Yes, there was a stone staircase opposite the wooden ladder. The storeroom was quiet; *tufo*, the volcanic rock from which it was built, erases noise. In a corner was a bedspring, a mattress, some books, a Bible. There was even a toilet, the kind you had to squat over. I climbed back up saddened. I hadn't discovered a thing.

. . .

It didn't cross my mind, it never could, to tell the police. To betray a secret, reveal a hiding place, are things a child doesn't do. In childhood spying on someone is despicable. Not even a discarded thought, it never occurred to me. I went down to the storeroom often that August, I liked the cool and rested silence of the tufo. I started reading the books, sitting on the ladder where the light came in. Not the Bible, God was too scary. That's how I picked up the habit of reading. The first was called *The Three Musketeers*, but there were four of them. At the top of the ladder, feet dangling, my head learned to draw light from books. When I finished them I wanted more.

Down the alley where I lived were the shops of the book vendors who sold to students. Outside they kept used books on sale in wooden boxes. I started going there, to pick out a book and sit down on the ground to read. One man chased me away. I went to another and he let me stay. A good man, Don Raimondo, who needed no words to understand. He gave me a stool so I wouldn't have to read on the ground. Then he told me he would lend me the book if I brought it back to him without damaging it. I replied thank you, I would bring it back the next day. I spent all night finishing it. Don Raimondo saw that I kept my word and let me take home a book a day.

I would choose the thin ones. I picked up the habit in summer when there was no teacher to teach me new things. They weren't books for children, many words in the middle I did not understand, but the end, the end I understood. It was an invitation to escape.

· · ·

Ten years later I found out from Don Gaetano that a Jewish guy had hidden in the storeroom in 1943. I was in my last year of school and Don Gaetano had started to confide in me. In the afternoons he would teach me how to play scopa, to figure out the unmatched cards. He used to win. He didn't throw his card down on the table, he played quickly, delayed by my mental count of the cards that had been played. To reciprocate our newfound familiarity, I decided to tell him something.

"Don Gaetano, one summer ten years ago I went downstairs, to the big room with the boxes."

"I know."

"How do you know?"

"I know everything that happens here. The dust, *guaglio'*, the wooden ladder was covered with dust and hand- and footprints. Only you could have slipped in there, between the legs of Ruggero. They used to call you *'a scigna*."

"And you didn't say anything to me?"

"You're the one who said nothing. I kept an eye on you, you went down cellar, didn't touch the boxes, and didn't tell anyone."

"I didn't have anyone."

"What did you go down there to do?"

"I like the darkness and there were books. That's where I picked up the habit of reading."

"A monkey with books: you climbed up that pipe as quick as a mouse, you dove between feet to get the ball, you had a natural courage, unforced."

"No one told me to do one thing or another. I learned at school what was allowed. I'm happy to go, I thank my foster mother for making me study. This is my last year, then the scholarship she got me runs out."

"You're getting a lot out of school. You're *roba buona*, good stuff."

. . .

That was his ultimate compliment, *roba buona*, a noble title for him.

"But at scopa you're a mozzarella."

"Let me ask, Don Gaetano, what was the use of the tilted ladder that came out behind the statue? No one could pass through there."

"Yes they could. During the war I sawed through one of Ruggero's legs, in an emergency you could remove it. During the war we needed hiding places, for contraband, for guns, for people who had to hide. A hunt was on for Jews, the money was good. In the city there weren't very many."

Don Gaetano noticed my curiosity about stories that had taken place around the time of my birth. He forgave the inhabitants, war brought out the worst in people, but not the informers, anyone who had sold a Jew to the police. "*È 'na carogna*"—He's a dirty rat. "The Jews, aren't they the same as us? They don't believe in Jesus Christ, and I don't either. They're people like us, born and raised here, they speak dialect. With the Germans however we had nothing in common. They wanted to boss us around, in the end they put people up against the wall and shot them, looted the stores. But when the time came and the city went after them, they ran like us, they lost all their bluster. What did the Jews ever do to the Germans? We never did figure it out. Our people didn't even know there was such a thing as Jews, a people from antiquity. But when the chance to make some money was involved, everyone knew who was Jewish. If a reward had been offered for phoenixes, some of us would have found them, even secondhand. Because there were rats who were informers.

· · ·

Our card games were interrupted by people who passed by the doorman's loge, asked for something, dropped off, picked up. Nothing escaped Don Gaetano. It was an old building complex with various apartment blocks, he knew everyone's business. People would come by to ask his advice. Don Gaetano would tell me to watch the door and then go. When he came back he would pick up his cards and the conversation where he had left off.

"He stayed down there until the Americans arrived and until the last day he thought I might sell him to the Germans. That's what his old doorman had done. He had managed to escape by the roof, with just enough time to slip on a pair of pants and a shirt, no shoes. He had a parcel of books within reach and brought them along. Jews are taught to run at an early age, like us, with the earthquake always beneath our feet and the volcano ready to blow. But we don't run away from the house carrying books."

"I would, Don Gaetano, I'll bring along my school-books if I have to run from an earthquake."

"He came to me at night under an air raid. I kept the main door open and he slipped in. He had torn from his chest the star he was supposed to keep sewn on, threads were hanging from his lapel. I took him down there, he stayed for a month, the worst month of the war. At the point of the uprising I brought him a pair of shoes I'd stolen from a German soldier. With them on he came out to meet the liberated city. He asked me why I hadn't sold him out."

"And what did you answer?"

"What could I answer? He had spent a month down there counting the minutes wondering if he'd be saved or not. Every thank-you he uttered to me was laced with suspicion. The war was about to end, the Americans had arrived in Capri. Angrier still was the thought of being arrested a few days before free-dom. That September was a furnace. The Germans planted mines up and down the seashore to prevent

an American landing, they blew up whole chunks of
the city, and the air raids went on and on. The sea
suddenly filled with hundreds of American ships. Fire
coming at us from every side. For us it was about stealing freedom, for him it was about his life. And his life
was hanging from someone who could betray him or
be arrested, murdered, and not come back to him with
something to eat. When he heard me descending the
stairs he didn't know whether it was me or the end."

"What did you answer him, why didn't you sell him
out?"

"Because I don't sell human flesh. Because war brings
out the worst in people but also the best. Because he
had come shoeless, who knows why? I don't remember what I answered him, maybe I didn't. History had
ended and the whys didn't matter. I heard his thoughts
and I answered, but he couldn't hear mine. You can't
speak with other people's thoughts, they're deaf."

"So it's true what they say about you, Don Gaetano,
that you hear the thoughts in people's heads?"

"It is and it isn't, sometimes yes and sometimes no.
Better this way because people have evil thoughts."

"If I think of something can you guess it?"

"No, *guaglio'*, I get the thoughts off the top of someone's head, the ones someone doesn't even know he

has. If you set about studying your own business, it stays with you. But thoughts are like sneezes, they escape all of a sudden and I hear them."

That's how he knew everyone's business, that's why he had a sadness ready for the worst and a crooked smile to throw it away. From the corners of his eyes the wrinkles opened and the melancholy drained out.

"Was the Jewish guy thinking a lot?"

"Yes, he was. Not when he was reading, but the rest of the time, yes, about the Holy Land, about a ship to get there. Europe is lost to us, here there is no life. He gave the example of a belt. We Jews, he thought, are a belt around the waist of the world. With the holy book we are the leather strip that has been holding up the trousers ever since Adam realized he was naked. Many times the world has wanted to take the belt off and throw it away. It feels too tight.

"I remember that thought clearly, he often had it. When he came out into the open air he could barely stand on his own two feet. He went to his home but it had been occupied. A family had settled there, they'd even changed the lock. I went there to put in a word and they moved out, but first they emptied the house, they even tore the electric wires from the walls."

"How did you persuade them?"

"We had guns, we had fought the Germans. I went at night, fired at the lock, went in and told them I would be back at noon and wanted to find the house empty. That's how it went. He moved back into his house, sold it a few months later, and went abroad, to Israel. He came by the loge to say good-bye. The city was still a pile of rubble. 'I'm bringing a stone from Naples with me. I'm going to put it in the wall of the house I'll have in Israel. There we will build with the stones they've thrown at us.'"

. . .

I would listen, play scopa, lose. In the evenings I jotted down Don Gaetano's stories. The city was school, too. I was sorry when the summer lessons ended. The students were happy, not me. I found consolation in Don Raimondo's books, yellowed paper he would rescue when someone wanted to get rid of some books.

"A person takes a lifetime to fill up the shelves and a child can't wait to empty them and throw everything away. What do they put on the empty shelves, provolone? All I want is for you to get them out of here, they tell me. And there lies a person's life, his impulses, expenses, sacrifices, satisfaction at seeing his learning grow by inches, like a plant."

"Don Raimondo, how will I ever repay you, you let me read without buying."

"Think nothing of it. You bring them back to me dusted off. When you're a man you'll come to me to buy them."

. . .

The city in the summer feels lighter, at night it goes out to the alleyways to breathe. With Don Gaetano I played scopa in the courtyard without winning a hand.

"*T'aggia 'impara' e t'aggia perdere.*" This was his sentence at the end of the game. "Once I've taught you I'll have to lose you." It was a fact, that's how things had to go. The same would happen with the city, it too had to teach me and then let me go. At game's end I would go back to my little room to hold on to the things I'd learned. Odd, the Jew's thought about the belt. I checked my own, it wasn't tight, I let it out one notch anyway. Even if the world believed the belt was too tight, it couldn't get rid of it. Backward, to before the holy book, it could not go. I had read that the world was jealous of the Jews because they had been chosen. In the war they had been chosen as the target. The man confined below the city sent news even from there. When he left his hiding place, why hadn't he taken his books, not even the Bible?

"I told him that he was forgetting his package. He replied that it might be useful to someone else. Even the Bible? He told me a verse that was written inside: Naked came I out of my mother's womb, and naked shall I return there. As if to say that for him the hideout was the place of his second birth. He had to leave without baggage."

"Don Gaetano, were you hiding a saint?"

"He was no saint, I overheard him quarreling with the heavenly father, telling him that his faith was a prison sentence. We are marked by circumcision, we bear the condemnation inscribed on our bodies. Our creator took away his breath and left us as mud. That's what he called the heavenly father, our creator. He wasn't a saint. He was someone who quarreled with that creator of his."

"So then you are the saint, risking your life to save a stranger."

"Do you have to go looking for saints? There are neither saints nor devils. There are some people who perform some good deeds and many evil ones. Any moment is right to do something good, but to do something evil takes opportunity, convenience. War is the best opportunity to do rotten things. It grants permission. To do a good deed requires no permission."

. . .

A peddler came into the courtyard, Don Gaetano stuck his head out, showed his face, said hello. There were frequent visits from *'o sapunaro*, the used-goods man, with a cart he pulled himself. Greater in girth than height, he wasn't happy until heads were sticking out of every apartment. He had a voice that could raise the dead. Don Gaetano had a nickname for him: Judgment Day. He would bring him a bottle of water and between one holler and the next the man would empty it.

"Don Gaeta', *v'arricurdate ncopp' e barricade 'e via Foria?*"—Do you remember being on the Via Foria barricades?

It was his calling card. He and two women had turned over a streetcar in the middle of a big road to stop the German tanks.

"*Nuie siamo robba bona*"—We're made of good stuff.

Don Gaetano could tell how the economy was doing by looking at the used-goods man's cart, the things that people threw away.

"Everyone is rich nowadays, throwing away bathtubs, no less, they even throw away wool mattresses, they buy the kind with springs. They throw away pedal-operated sewing machines. They believe in electricity like eternal life, and if it runs out?"

. . .

It was an angry summer, almost cold. In July the top of the volcano turned white. People played its numbers in the lottery and up they came, promptly. There were big wins. The year before a cobbler had nailed four out of five. I asked Don Gaetano whether thoughts with numbers ever came to him. He made a gesture as if to brush away a fly. But was there an art to it? Could you learn to hear people's thoughts?

"First of all, don't call them people, they're persons, each and every one. If you call them people you lose sight of the person. You can't hear the thoughts of people, but of persons, one at a time."

He was right, until that age I hadn't noticed persons, it was all one people. At the loge that summer I learned to recognize the tenants. As a child the only one who mattered to me was on the third floor behind the window, I didn't even know what her parents looked like. She had disappeared, and after that getting to know the building's other tenants didn't much matter to me.

. . .

"So there's no way of learning to be like you, Don Gaetano? There isn't an art to it?"

"Even if there was, I wouldn't tell you. It's not nice to know what crosses the minds of persons. So many bad intentions come and go that are not acted on. If I say what one person thinks of another, all hell will break loose."

"So you hear and don't intervene?"

"Sometimes I get in the middle. You've heard about the time it snowed and so many people played the snow's numbers in the lotto it almost broke the bank: a guy that lived in a *basso* at the bottom of the alley picked the right numbers and said nothing to his wife. I called him out and said: this isn't right. 'What?' he says. You don't just bring debts home: you also bring good news."

"And what did he do?"

"He went to buy goat, wine, and he showed up with his winnings."

"But something you could have used, an overheard thought that might come in handy?"

Don Gaetano gave me a dark look. "If you found a wallet would you give it back to the person who lost it?"

"It's never happened to me, I don't know. To give you an answer with no experience to back it up, I would have to say yes. But I'll only know if it happens to me. I can't know beforehand how I would act."

"You're honest. When I find a useful thought belonging to someone else, I don't pocket it. I leave it there. I can't give it back saying: do you realize you've lost a thought, and then act like I hadn't heard it."

"I wish I knew other people's thoughts."

"You? You can't even guess the three unplayed cards from the last hand of scopa. First learn to play."

. . .

Don Gaetano was familyless, too. Raised in an orphanage, then a seminary, he was supposed to become a priest. But they say he fell in love with a streetwalker and decided to defrock. For twenty years he was far away, in Argentina. He came back in 1940, just in time for the war. This is what I knew about him before the summer of our familiarity.

"You used to have a crush on the little girl on the third floor. You were always looking in that direction."

"I was trying to get her to notice me, the way children do. But one day she suddenly disappeared. Do you know where she and her family went?"

"I know where she is now. She's come back to Naples and she's going out with a young guy, a gangster who's locked up. She's not for you."

The return of that lonely age, the thought of myself as a child searching for her face behind the glass, climbing the stairs in the hope of running into her: I moved my fingers to the bridge of my nose to catch the two rebel tears escaping. In childhood bonds get forged that never break apart. That night I wrote Don Gaetano's sentence: First learn to play. Then what? If I learned to play scopa, would I then be able to hear thoughts? I couldn't ask, that one sentence had to be enough.

· · ·

When it was Don Gaetano's turn to be a child, no one in the orphanage told stories, so it was up to him. Around the little stove in the dormitory, he made up lives of animals, kings, wanderers. The children were warmed and nourished through their ears. He would tell the stories in dialect.

"Neapolitan is deliberate, you say something and they believe you. In Italian there is doubt: did I understand correctly? Italian is good for writing, where you don't need a voice, but to tell a story you need our language, which glues the story together and makes you visualize it. Neapolitan is for storytelling, it opens your ears and your eyes. I used to tell the children about life outside. No one used to come to see us, not even on Sundays. When a child grows up without a caress, its skin hardens, it feels nothing, not even a beating. The ears are all that's left to learn the world. By us there was plenty of shouting, but no one cried. Outside the children cried, inside the orphanage no one knew how. Not even when one of us died, it was an everyday occurrence. The fever would come, burn, and extinguish. When it was cold we would pile up, *'o muntone*, we called it. We would all huddle in a single embrace. We would take turns, those on the outside would move inside. We would create heat and have some laughs. All it took was for one person to shout *'O muntone* and right away we would make a mound, everyone piled up."

. . .

"The big windows at the orphanage looked inward to the courtyard, the streetside windows were walled up, some of us had jumped down to run away. I was the only one who could climb over the gate at night. I was as light as you, I wandered the city, mingling with the crowd that moves at night. I would go to the seashore, I liked the ships. When I was about thirteen I became friends with a prostitute who was my same age. I would do her favors, warn her if there was any police movement. When she was done and I had to go back, she paid me with a cup of milk and a brioche. We resembled each other, a brother and sister who were getting together. Then she met a guy who married her and she left for the North. The city is beautiful at night. There's danger but also freedom. The sleepless wander about: artists, murderers, gamblers. The taverns, fry-shacks, and cafes stay open. Those who make their living at night say hello, get to know each other. People indulge their vices. The light of day accuses, the dark of night absolves. Out come the transformed, men dressed as women, because nature bids them to and no one harasses them. At night no one asks for explanations. Out come the crippled, the blind, the lame, who in the daylight are rejected. It's a pocket pulled inside out, night in the city. Out come the dogs, too, the strays. They wait for the night to sift through the garbage, so many dogs manage to survive on their own. At night the city is a civil place."

. . .

"I had quicksilver in my legs, I ran everywhere, satisfied my hunger. They say it's the legs, not the teeth, that feed the wolf. By day I put the quicksilver into telling stories to children. No one in there had a name, we would make them up. One kid was *Muorzo*, Bite, because he had no teeth. A lame kid was called *'O Treno 'e Foggia*, the Foggia Train, because he always arrived late, one was *Suonno*, Sleep, because he was always asleep on his feet, one was *Sisco*, Whistle, because he whistled like a peddler, I was *'O Nonno*, Grandpa, the oldest. Many of them had never seen the sea, I would tell them about it: it was a seesaw of water, the ships played on top of it, passing from one wave to the next. I helped them visualize the waves with a bedsheet.

"For those of us inside, the way to get an education was the seminary. So I entered one. I used to run away from there at night, too."

. . .

On summer evenings people walked down the street to catch a breath by the seashore. It wasn't the nocturnal city Don Gaetano knew, which began later, when

the promenade was over. The two of us in the courtyard taking in the fresh air after a game of scopa, we
were quiet for a while, spoke for a stretch. To counter the day he thought back to the violent summer of
1943. He had to lower his voice in the emptiness so it
wouldn't echo through the courtyard.

"Before seeing him standing there shoeless and
with books under his arm, I had no thought of hiding
anyone. Down cellar I kept a little bit of contraband
and lately the guns commandeered from the police.
But when I saw him at the entry I pulled him inside.
I would go to see him during the air raids, when the
building emptied in the dash for the shelters. I stayed
back to keep an eye on things, under the bombs the
marauders were on the loose, burgling houses. They
weren't afraid of anything, and bombs were being
dropped on the city like crazy. I would visit him during the alert, so he would have someone to talk to.
Down cellar the war made a muffled sound, the bombs
were the pounding of a person who knocks on the
door, the tufo absorbed the noise and withstood the
impact without vibrations. The bombs broke things
up but didn't make the walls shake. Tufo is antiaircraft
material."

. . .

"What did you use to say to each other down there?"

"We would play scopa. I taught him, he was a fast learner. He didn't want to lose, unlike you, who don't care. I liked his tenacity. A guy who had lost everything, whose life was hanging from a nail, from a stranger, would dig in his heels so he wouldn't lose at scopa. He was a guy who took everything seriously.

"'You're too serious for a Neapolitan,' I used to tell him. He would reply, 'Since when? Down here I laugh my head off. Outside is the war, the massacre of my people, the collapse of the city in which I was born, and I'm down here as if I was waiting under a doorway for a storm to pass. And you're here, too, coming to keep me company. I read the holy book, our prophets, and I start to laugh. Down here, the year of grace 1943 for you and the year 5704 for us, it makes for comic reading. I'm not serious, Don Gaetano, I'm tragic, a reject from comedy. Let me at least take seriously the game of scopa, which is almost a religious art. Yes, religious: the most important card is the seven, which is the number of our novelty as Jews. It was the Jews who invented the seven-day week. Before the calendars used to go according to the moon and sun. Then our divinity let us know that the days were six plus one. We sanctified the number before scopa did. There are forty cards in a deck, like the years spent in the desert, between the exodus from Egypt and the entrance to the promised land. And then there's the *spariglio*, a variant on taking a card with a card of equal value. You can take it with a combination of cards that add up to the same number. This is an invention that doesn't exist in nature. Nature goes in pairs, scopa goes by *spariglio*. It's in the dealer's interest, not the player's, to keep everything even, *apparigliato*. It's a fight between order and chaos. Let me at least take scopa seriously.'"

. . .

"When he spoke to me like this, it shut me up and gave me the shivers."

"I'm getting them too just from hearing you remember his words. I have to write them down the same day so I don't lose them. You can still remember them almost twenty years later."

"It has to do with the game. If you can remember *carte sparigliate* you can do the same thing with your thoughts. I would come back upstairs from these visits in a daze. Outside it was September 1943, and down there it was a month from the Jewish calendar in the year 5704. Down there was a man who came from an ancient time, a contemporary of Moses and the pharaohs, and the lot had fallen on him to be a contemporary of the Nazis. It's a good thing I didn't hear him laughing down there. 'Don Gaetano, let me know when you see the stars in broad daylight.' Outside the youths stole guns from the barracks and hid them. A group that had one guy in a military police uniform had emptied the armory of the Sant'Elmo fortress. In the meantime the Germans ransacked the churches and blew up the San Rocco bridge in Capodimonte. The Sanità bridge we managed to save by disconnecting the explosive charges, we did the same with the aqueduct. They wanted to leave behind a city in ruins. The uprising was its salvation.

"The bad came with the good. A good person might start loan-sharking, a girl from a good family start to prostitute herself to the Germans. A guy reputed to be a gangster would be the first to run for the shelter. The Germans were even more craven because the war was going badly. The landing in Salerno had succeeded. They blew up the factories, looted the warehouses to leave them empty. In the last days of September the hunger and exhaustion in people's faces made the city frightening. Those who still had something ate in secret. The Germans put on a show: they would break down the door to a shop, then invite the people in to ransack it. When the crowd lunged forward they would shoot into the air and film the scene. It was for their propaganda: the German soldier intervenes to prevent looting. These are things that happened, *guaglio'*, on one of these same beautiful September days."

. . .

Sitting on two chairs in the courtyard we were looking up to where the city ended and who knows what began, maybe the universe. It was close by, a piazza enclosed by a circle of railings. Don Gaetano stared with his hands entwined and breathed deeply. I twisted my neck back, too: the field beyond the balconies moved in a circle, very slowly, but it still made your head spin.

Eyes that on the ground didn't go beyond a ray of the horizon were able to see the planets. No wonder the sky went to your head, it made you believe you could go there.

"They were dropping bombs every night, the city was always on the run, it didn't scream, it ran and saved its breath. The explosions of German bombs were confounded with the American bombings, the sirens sounded after the antiaircraft artillery had started firing."

Then he would remember some odd event and a smile would come to his face. "A young guy was strolling arm in arm with a girl when the siren went off. He couldn't run off by himself and leave her behind, and she couldn't run in high heels, so there was a scene of him pulling her and her behind him screaming at the top of her lungs: let me go, let me go. But with him nothing doing, he was forced to drag her. The girls were braver. Later the guys redeemed themselves with the days in late September. It takes special moments for men to show their valor. Women are more valiant on a normal basis, if you could call anything about 1943 normal."

. . .

"People came out of the shelters after the air raids and found their houses gone. The faces of those who from one hour to the next had lost everything: an old man was sitting atop the ruins of his building staring at the sky. He came to me and said, '*Sto gradanno 'ncielo pe vvede' addo' me pozzo sistema'. Ccà 'nterra nun tengo cchiù niente*'—I'm looking at the sky to see where

I can settle. Because on the earth I have nothing left. People searched through the rubble of their homes for something to salvage. They rummaged from one room to the next going through the doorways, even if the walls were gone, entering the kitchen to see if they had turned the gas off, then they would look up and see the sky coming through the ceiling. The insolent sky of September 1943: a tablecloth with embroidered borders, fresh and clean without a speck of dust, a stain. An unblinking turquoise: come down to earth for a while, sky, let's trade places, why don't you take up there all the filth and spread your tablecloth down here on earth. A vicious, distant sky—not like today—that started from the rooftops. The uprising began when it started to rain. It's as if the city was waiting for an agreed sign or the sky was closing. And the Americans stopped bombing."

. . .

"The Jewish guy asked me what was going on with the weather. I answered that nothing was going on, it wasn't changing and it wasn't letting a drop fall on the dust. There wasn't enough water and the women went to the sea with buckets so they could at least do the laundry. Not even the Jewish guy liked the weather settling into a nice unchanging pattern. He used to ask me whether you could see any stars by day, he was waiting for a sign.

"'People like sunny days, to me they're frightening. The worst things happen under sunny skies. When the weather is bad a person prefers to postpone an evil deed. With the sun anything can happen. If I make it to autumn, I want to start dancing under a cloudburst.

"'By autumn the war will have passed, the Americans are in Salerno.'

"I didn't tell him they were in sight, he might have done something crazy like going out. I could hear his thoughts. 'So close to freedom and unable to see it, cooped up down here wondering whether it's salvation or a trap. The door opens and down they come to take me.' Not even in his thoughts did he want to imagine I could betray him. If not me, then someone from the building who had caught on. He wondered whether anyone knew of the hiding place. My assurances could not be enough for him.

"'These are not good times for trust and I'm not asking you to trust me. I'm telling you not to let bad ideas get the better of you, don't come out looking for a safe place, there isn't one. If you do come out they'll shoot you on sight. Commander Scholl has issued a bulletin, all men between the ages of eighteen and thirty-three have to report to the barracks or they'll be shot. Of the three thousand expected, one hundred twenty showed up.'

"Do you see what kind of a war it was, *guaglio'*? More unarmed people were dying than soldiers. On the streets I started to hear people's thoughts: why are they remaining in the city and not going off to fight? Why are they beating up on the poor rather than going to the front? The thoughts began from a single head. When persons become a people it's shocking. So a morning came, a late September Sunday, when it finally rained and on everyone's lips I heard the same words, spat out by the same thought: *mo' basta*—enough already. It was a wind coming not from the sea but from inside the city: *mo' basta, mo' basta.* If I closed my ears I could hear it louder. The city was sticking its head out of the bag. *Mo' basta, mo' basta.* A drumbeat called and out came the *guaglioni* with guns. The center of the uprising was the Liceo Sannazzaro, the students were the first. Then out came the men hidden beneath the city. They climbed up from underground like a resurrection. '*Dalle 'n cuollo, 'dagli addosso*'—Jump 'em, let 'em have it—the streets were blocked by the barricades. In the Vomero district they cut down the sycamores and used them to make roadblocks against the tanks. We made a barricade on Via Foria, fitting together about thirty streetcars. The city sprang like a trap. Four days and three nights, it was like today, the end of September."

. . .

"The German tanks managed to pass the Via Foria blockade, make it down to Piazza Dante, and head toward Via Roma. There they were stopped. Giuseppe Capano, age fifteen, slipped between the tracks of a tank, set off a hand grenade, and managed to escape out the back before the explosion. Assunta Amitrano, age seventeen, dropped from the fourth floor a marble slab taken from a bureau and smashed the machine gun on a tank. Luigi Mottola, age fifty-one, sewer repairman, set off a gas canister while popping out of a manhole cover under the belly of a tank. A student at the conservatory, Ruggero Semeraro, age seventeen, opened the balcony and started playing on the piano the Marseillaise, music that instills even more courage. Antonio La Spina, priest, age sixty-seven, from the barricade in front of the bank of Naples, shouted out Psalm 94, the psalm of revenge. Santo Scapece, barber, age thirty-seven, threw a bucket of soapsuds through the peephole of a tank that ended up crashing into the gates of a flower shop. Our fellow citizens developed infallible aim in the space of three days. The burning bottles wreaked havoc on the tanks, blinding them with flames. I became an expert at making them, I would put soap flakes inside to make the fire stick better. The diesel fuel was donated by the Mergellina fishermen, who couldn't go out to sea because of the blockading and mining of the harbor.

"Six persons in the midst of the ready crowd came up with the right moves to create trouble for an armored division of the powerful army that had single-handedly conquered half of Europe. It wasn't the first time six persons had carried off such a feat. Already in 1799 the French army, the most powerful of that era, had been stopped at the entrance to the city by a popular insurrection after the dissolution of the Bourbon army. Six persons endowed with first name, last name, age, and profession, were stopping the Germans from retaking the city. Six persons whose names had been drawn at random by necessity decided the situation, while all around them others made many generous but inexact moves. When six persons appear, all at once, then you win."

. . .

"And where is that populace today, Don Gaetano?"

"Back in its place, it hasn't moved and it hasn't forgotten. The populace makes its move, then immediately it breaks up, it goes back to being a crowd of persons who rush back to their own affairs, but with more energy, because uprisings fire up the spirits of those caught up in them. The fighting on the third day was fiercer. We also had to drive out the Fascists, who were shooting down at us from the rooftops. In the midst of those battles I was able to go down to the hiding place to bring him something to eat. The third day I dropped by to see him at dawn. I told him if I wasn't back in twenty-four hours, he could go out. He asked me to do him a favor that day.

"'Go to the seashore and cast a stone in the water for me.' I thought he'd gone soft in the head from being down there. I answered that I didn't know if I would be going to the seaside, that the city was in revolt. 'It's one of our rituals, tomorrow for us is the New Year. We celebrate in September. By casting the stone in the water we make the gesture to be delivered from sin. The year for us begins tomorrow. Ours would have it that today is the day before happiness.'

"He hadn't gone soft. Before stopping by the up-rising's command center to take my orders, I went down to Santa Lucia where the women were fetching water. I climbed over the rocks and I cast a nice heavy stone into the sea. It was New Year for the Jews and it should be New Year for us, too. On that day the city shot off its best fireworks, the shots of freedom. The Germans retreated, pursued and targeted from every rooftop and street corner. They shot the last cannon shots from Capodimonte. One landed in front of the entry to our building and exploded downward. In the hiding place the Jewish guy was thrown from his cot and got a head wound. To dress it he tore up his shirt. I found him there that night when I brought him the news that the Germans were gone.

"'You won?' He didn't believe me.

"'You won, too.'

"'It's the first war we've won since the time of Judas Maccabaeus. And also your city, it's the first time it's won a war.'

"'It's also the first time you've fractured your skull falling off the bed.'

"He asked me whether I'd cast the stone into the sea. Yes, I replied, this way it's New Year for the whole city. I treated his wound. I had a bottle of brandy to celebrate the end of the war, I used it to clean the cut. We drank a couple of glasses, our heads were spinning. I had to crawl up the stairs.

"The next day the city was free. The Germans made an attempt to come back but they were stopped and gave up. He came out leaning against me with his eyes closed. With the bandages on his head he was a man emerging from the land of the dead. The city was in ruins, we went to the seashore. The American warships were like so many gray rocks jutting out in the middle of the bay. He leaned against me and stamped his feet on the ground in a pair of German shoes. 'I don't want to walk on tiptoe anymore.' On Via Caracciolo the first jeeps drove by with the star painted on the hood. 'The stars did battle, as is written in the Song of Deborah, here are the stars in broad daylight.'

"'Open your eyes now, just a little, a peek.'

"He placed a hand over his forehead and saw the arrival of freedom passing by.

"'You're free,' I said, and we hugged each other. Everyone was hugging. The day before happiness, we almost missed it."

While Don Gaetano was talking I was gazing at the third-floor window. The day before happiness had not yet arrived for me. I wanted to know it. I didn't want it to happen all of a sudden and not to notice it the day before. They knew it was supposed to happen the day after. I spent the rest of the night in my room, jotting down Don Gaetano's story.

. . .

In summer I wake up early, I go down to the Santa Lucia rocks with a net to look for sea urchins and if I'm lucky maybe an octopus. I stay for a couple of hours, before the sun surmounts the shoulders of the volcano. On their way home from some all-night party, the rich are leaving the private clubs. In evening wear exposed to the early light, they rush for cover together with bats running late. Also on his way home is the count who lives in my building and gambles away his possessions at the tables of his club. He doesn't see me. The eyesight of the rich is different from ours, we need to see everything. They only see what they want. I roll my pants up to my knees and climb down the rocks. I lower my net into the water and pull it up, letting it drag across the surface of the rocks. A stroke of luck and I find something to bring to the table. Before going home I stop by Don Raimondo's to give him back the book. He helps me find another, his choice.

Don Raimondo is an adventurous bookseller, he rescues libraries, even from the trash heap. Most of the time he's called to a house in mourning that is clearing out the space of the deceased.

"More than clothes and shoes, books bear their imprint. The heirs get rid of them to exorcise the ghost, to get rid of it. The excuse is that space is needed, the books are suffocating. But what do they put in their place, to cover the walls marked by their outline?"

Don Raimondo tells me what he can't tell them. "The emptiness on the surface of a wall left by a sold bookshelf is the deepest I know. I take away with me the banished books, I give them a second life. Like the second coat in painting, used for finishing, a book's second life is its best." He's rescued the library of a lover of American literature. "I'm reading great adventures from the place where so many Neapolitans went to live. But you can tell they don't write books."

The names of American writers are always American names. They have a sporty way of life: a person has to pull himself up by his bootstraps. It seems that no one has family, the only relationship is marriage. Or else their books are all written by orphans.

. . .

With Don Gaetano one afternoon I went to see a war-time bomb being defused. A lot of them had dropped without exploding. The workers digging a new basin found one in the harbor. We weren't allowed to go near but Don Gaetano knows the back alleys and we were able to watch from a good vantage point. All the while he kept telling his stories of the days of freedom.

"The Fascists had disappeared. There wasn't a black shirt in sight, they had all been dyed gray. It was the color of *nuncepenzammocchiù*—we're not going to think about it anymore. In Naples they forget the bad as soon as a little good arrives. And they're right. A nice round of applause for the Americans and then we carry on with our business. But we were the ones who deserved applause from them, for having cleared the field. With them I started to dig up bombs. I brought you along today to show you because this used to be my job. There were lots of them, stuck in the strangest places. One in ten hadn't exploded on impact. I even removed some from the cemetery. We would dig all around it, then the bomb squad expert came to defuse it or, in really bad cases, to set it off. I did it for a year, it paid well. Between us workers we used to call them eggs. They were the eggs of war left behind to hatch.

"Some exploded while the rubble was being moved. With a blow of the pickax a worker loosened a stone that gave just the right tap to the fuse. And so the war lived on in eggs that hatched later. Not even a finger could be found. The shifted air killed the guy next to him, too. It destroyed his internal organs. Outside he looked healthy, inside he was a mess. I'm telling you these things so that one day, if you become president and they want to make you sign your name to a war, and you've uncapped your pen and are about to put your signature on the paper, all at once you will re-member these events and maybe, who knows, you will say: I'm not signing."

. . .

"Me, president? I can't even put two words together."

"Yes, you. Why not? You know how to listen. This is the prime quality of someone who has to speak."

"Don Gaetano, you're confusing me, I'll never give orders to anyone, but I will never forget your words. Didn't it frighten you to work with bombs?"

"Nowadays I wouldn't do it. In those days you felt you had a duty to help put the destruction behind us.

I was right for the job, I didn't have anyone. No one would have grieved for me. It's a thought that makes you lighter. With me there were heads of households who had to earn their wages with shaking knees. With each blow of the pickax they called out to their saints. Some of them were doing the work because valuable stuff could be found under the rubble. When something precious turned up you were supposed to give a shout and hand it over to the foreman. It was the rule of war, profiteers had hell to pay, but some guys took the chance anyway and hid stuff."

. . .

From our perch on the bluff you could see the tail end of the bomb. There was a guy in uniform bustling about.

"He does the defusing. You can tell the fuses are in good shape, not rusty. When you unscrew it there's the risk of a spark. Once a bomb was stuck inside an elevator shaft. You couldn't demolish the surrounding wall, you had to be lowered from above and defuse. The American explosives expert didn't want anything to do with it. I volunteered, I knew the system. If you pay me what he gets, I'll go. They lowered me with a rope and I did the unscrewing and extracting. It was as quiet as a hideout. It was winter but down there it was warm. I was stuck between the bomb and the elevator cables, but comfortable. They had cleared the building, they were waiting for me. I relaxed, it was better if I took longer, to make it seem more difficult. I nodded off and when I woke up I didn't know where I was. Two hours had gone by, I pulled the rope and they hoisted me up, very slowly, since I was holding the fuse in my arms."

· · ·

In front of us the explosives expert was shimmying up and down the bomb's back. I saw Ahab on Moby Dick.

"Don't think bad thoughts," said Don Gaetano, who had heard.

"He's got it." We saw the man stand up and walk away with something in his arms. We went back home. It was a Sunday afternoon in September, the crowd went down to the shore to breathe good air. We walked uphill to the alley. We turned around to see the city before wandering home. In the middle of the bay an American aircraft carrier was anchored, surrounded by a hundred small sailboats racing each other between the buoys. The sea was all around but they were crowded into a small space. Don Gaetano's stories were abundant, too, and they fit inside a single person. He used to say it was because he had lived below, and stories are water that flows to the bottom of the slope. Man is a basin that collects stories, the lower he is the more he receives.

In the building they started asking Don Gaetano, "Did you hire an assistant?" I delivered the mail, filled in for him when he had to make a service call to an apartment.

Don Gaetano knew how to do all kinds of repairs. He had a steady hand guided by sure instincts. Under his fingers the damage would disappear, it was nice to see. Even if the right material or tool was missing, he still did the repair.

"Don Gaeta', a draft comes in under the window, it gives me kidney problems, what do they call them, *i dulori areonautici*—airrenaulic pains—and that guy, the carpenter, doesn't want to come." The answer was emergency relief.

"Don't get discouraged, there's always a remedy. And if there isn't, does that mean when the handkerchief maker dies, we won't be able to blow our noses anymore? I'll be there in a second."

There was a more insolent version. "*È muorto chillo*

ca faceva i cànteri, e nun putimmo cchiù cacà"—The guy that made the chamber pots is dead, and we can't take a shit anymore. Don Gaetano preferred the handkerchief version. He would take a sheet of newspaper, wet it, then press it into the crack where the draft came through. It was better than putty.

. . .

I used to study at night, school was easy, I understood the subjects. They were boxes, what I put in, I found. At seventeen I didn't know any girls. I held in my thoughts the little girl on the third floor who with the passing years had grown up inside me. On the street I would look at the girls, searching for the one who might be her. She had multiplied into various possibilities. She was the destined one, but destiny can lose its way, it's not a sure thing that has to happen. Destiny is rare. One day I looked at the third floor and she was gone. A silence descended over my whole body. I spoke softly, breathed softly, walked on tiptoe, in response to the closed blinds the idea came to me to avoid making noise. The explorations, the search for buried treasure, also came to an end. You can see it was the third-floor window that drove me to adventure.

"You should have been born in the Middle Ages, in the times of the knights-errant," is what Don Gaetano, who could hear my thoughts, used to say.

But this is the Middle Ages, too, I would reply mentally. The city contains every era. The building and its tenants are the Middle Ages, which has slipped its legs into the trousers of the present. In the city they're still voting for the king: not the king of Savoia, they're voting for Ruggero the Norman.

. . .

There were regular interruptions of our afternoon games. The widow on the second floor used to ask Don Gaetano to come up, things needed fixing in her house. Don Gaetano would leave me in charge while he went upstairs with his toolkit. She was a beautiful woman whose hair was as dark as September blackberries. She dressed in full mourning and used to speak in a hoarse voice from behind her black veil. Another regular visit was from the count who was gambling away his possessions at the club. All he had left was the one apartment where he lived. His wife, a good seamstress, made clothing at home while he went out to gamble. He hadn't worked a day in his life.

"Never, Don Gaetano, never has a member of my family had to work for a living. Who am I to dishonor a family tradition?"

"May the day never come," Don Gaetano would reply.

"Does the boy know how to play cards—*E 'o guaglione sa giocare?*" he would ask.

"No, he's a mozzarella."

"What a shame, but you, you are in a class by yourself, I don't know a single player who's as good. Would you do me the honor of being my *scopone* partner? We'd break the bank at the club, the two of us."

There was no way it was going to happen, but the count would still insist.

"I'll cover any losses and we'll split the winnings. With you at the club I'll make a killing. Grant me the honor and the satisfaction."

Don Gaetano would defend himself by saying he wouldn't be allowed in a gentlemen's club, to make amends he would invite the count to play a hand with him in the loge. He knew it would never happen. The count, accustomed to this reply, would decline and say good-bye. In his wake he left a gust of aftershave that tickled the nose. Don Gaetano used to say the club was a cabal of crooks where dupes like the count were fleeced without realizing it. "They're so cunning they can steal your pants without removing your shoes."

. . .

Don Gaetano used to miss the nature he had gotten to know in Argentina. The plains where herds roamed freely, the lightning that struck "to the beat of the tarantella and the earth was the heavens' dance floor." "Being an orphan was natural, everyone was an orphan, animals and men on a plain as vast as an ocean. Bandits, defrocked priests, anarchists, Irishmen: Argentina relieved hearts of the burden behind the journey, gave room to the human will. The solitudes regulated your breath before the horizon. I had run away down there without knowing how to light a fire, Argentina taught me to stake my claim, to survive. Which is not the same as to live, to merely pass the time. Survival's goalpost is the end of the day, a good place to set up camp, water for the horse, and kindling for the fire.

"At first I was in Buenos Aires, teaching Latin to the children of rich emigrants, then I followed an Irishman who was traveling to the plains to raise sheep.

Then I broke away from him, too, and played the guest of nature and its abundant charity. I was worth one, the number assigned to each life, without any guarantee it would be saved. I could drop to zero any day, longevity had to be earned."

. . .

"On the plains of Argentina I became acquainted with fire. I saw it ignite under the thunderbolts, hide itself and slither under the cloudbursts. Then it would depart in the darting of a glowworm under folded grass, stick out its head, curl into a ball with the wind, hurl itself against a bush and dance on top of it. I saw it chase animals, seize birds in the air. I saw its orange back climb the hills, preceded by the trumpet of black smoke that races ahead of an attack."

When he spoke about Argentina Don Gaetano would use another language and a second, more throaty voice. The words that came out of him were more agitated, nervous, chomping at the bit.

"I would skirt the brushfires. The hunting was good but the main thing was that they fascinated me. The air was acrid, the eyebrows singed. The horse snorted in fear but the fire was proud and held fast. It leaves the earth black and white, sucks the marrow from the colors, depletes the green, blue, and brown. At night I headed back to camp, the flame I lit picked up the brushfire's scent and called out for it to come. At dawn I would snuff it out, trampling it to the last embers, and the fire hated me because I was its master, it couldn't stand the fact. It is a master of the ambush, suddenly bursting out on the opposite side, advancing even against the wind. It snarls when it's entrapped."

Don Gaetano's eyes became enchanted when he remembered.

"I had not been acquainted with fire. I was born when the volcano was emptying its force into heaven rather than earth. From the rooftops bagfuls of ashes were swept up. That's what I was told, that ash is heavy and makes ceilings collapse if it accumulates. Then I saw it again in Naples, lit up by the bombs. The bombs also crashed down from above like thunder, but they burned people and houses, not the plains.

"I didn't recognize it. It resembled men, it was isolated, rarely passed from one house to the next. I watched it rage, extinguish, leaving walls and even books still standing. Just some slight charring on the cover, it only consumed the title. Books are sea urchins, they stay closed and compact to withstand the fire. Bombardments are human fires, one of our imitations. I stared at it anyway, and wouldn't have made a move to put it out. Watch out for fire, *guaglio'*, because it calls, draws you close through enchantment and makes you dumb."

. . .

"It's over here that we're nothing, packed together in the alleys. Over there when my path crossed another man's, he was either a blood brother or a murderer. Argentina was the patria of refugees, anyone who had escaped from somewhere could stop watching his back.

"I traveled by horseback escorted by butterflies. Millions of butterflies flew close to the ground to let us run in their shadow. The carpet of their shadows fluttered around the horse's hooves, I rode on a flying plain. At night I would tie the animal to my leg if I couldn't find a tree or a rock. I would wake up in a new place, pulled by the horse looking for grass.

"In Argentina I forgot. Every new thing that I learned erased something from my earlier life. I started hearing people's thoughts. At first I took them for voices, I thought solitude had gone to my head. Then I found out they were the thoughts of others.

There was nothing I could do to shut them out. Knowing thoughts is being in the loge, in your pocket you carry the house keys, you're the gatekeeper. You know the sad thoughts, the troubles, the crimes. You're not the confessor, you can't absolve them. From the inside humanity is frightening, flesh to be roasted in hell. And you have to act as if you didn't know. Nature in Argentina is what made me what I am, it gave me its safe-conduct. Nature turns a boy into a man and you don't know it yet."

· · ·

I knew nothing of nature, of the body. I had grown up dry, hungry, my only release was the soccer games on Saturday afternoon and a practice session in the middle of the week. The sea was the Santa Lucia rocks, nature was what ended up in the net.

From time to time I would see the bay from the curve of a road on a hill. All that beauty, invisible to those who lived inside it, didn't seem possible. We were fish in the net and around us was the wide-open sea. I tried to find our alley but couldn't make it out, the streets were packed too close together. There we lived without knowing how much light and air was swirling one meter above the city. From the curve on the hill nature created a semicircle of land with Vesuvius in the middle. Nature existed if seen from a distance.

One Sunday Don Gaetano took me to the top of the volcano.

"You have to make his acquaintance, he's the master of the house, we are his tenants. Anyone born here has to pay him a visit."

. . .

We climbed past the broom trees, then over stony ground. We came to the edge of the crater, a mouth as wide as a lake, where the drizzle from the cloud evaporated before touching the ground. The summer cloud drenched us, covering us in sweat and rain. There was peace in this pillow of mist, a tense peace that centered the blood. On the volcano's edge, once the climb was over, I realized I had a hard-on. I walked away from Don Gaetano with the excuse I had to pee. A few steps downhill into the crater, I locked myself inside the density of the cloud and released my lust, scattering it over the compact ash. Don Gaetano called out to me and I found him. "It's nature, *guaglio'*, when you're alone in one of its forsaken spots and you know yourself." I was in a daze, the cloud had taken me into its bath, blown its steam in my face and held me inside. Open or closed my eyes saw the same thing, a veil over my lids and white blood that rose to the tip of my sex. It was nature and I was learning it for the first time. I had woken in a sweat other times, but inside the cloud I was the one doing the touching and pushing. On the way down we burst into the open air of the sun, which dried our clothes.

. . .

I brought to the table some fish I'd caught by dragging my net. Don Gaetano appreciated it and knew how to cook it. He made fun of me. "The same thing today, we're eating unlucky fish, the ones who had the misfortune of going for a stroll on your watch." He thought I needed experience at sea. He knew a fisherman at the Mergellina harbor who had moved to Ischia. He arranged for me to go on an outing with him. I got on board the last ferry of the day. From the dock next to us the emigrants were departing, I was going on a cruise. I was disoriented, with my hands in my lap, not knowing where to put them. The crossing confounded my senses, the smokestack blew squid ink against the setting sun, the engine's vibrations tickled my skin, my bites into a calzone broke me away from the city for the first time. I said good-bye with my eyes to the distance that was separating me. There is a farewell in those two hours of crossing, happy or sad I couldn't tell.

. . .

I landed on the island in the evening. At the dock a short stout man wearing a beret was waiting for me. He made me smile saying, "*Quanto si' lungo, vicini facimmo 'miccia e 'a bomba*"—Look how skinny you are, next to each other we're like a fuse and a bomb.

We went to the shore, pushed his boat in, and reached the open sea with the oars. It was an evening that widened the pores, wherever I cast my eyes I was amazed. No moon, the stars were enough to see in the distance. The island's lights were lost behind us. Above and ahead the sky abounded with galaxies. From the courtyard of our building you couldn't see how great a mass there was. Studied at school, the universe was the table set for guests with a telescope. Here it was hung out for the naked eye and it resembled the mimosa tree in March, blooming in clusters, bursting with uneven dots thrown haphazardly into the foliage, so dense they covered the trunk.

They descended all the way to the edges of the boat, I saw them between the oars and above the beret pulled over his head. That man, the fisherman, paid the heavens no mind. Could a man really get used to it? To being surrounded by stars and not even needing to shake them off? Thank you, thank you, thank you, said my eyes, for being there.

Farther out he said, "Give it a try," and handed me the oars. Long, to be pushed standing up, face to the prow. He told me to aim for a promontory. He started to unwind a long line from which every meter or so a sinker and some bait would drop.

I had seen the way he worked the oars and I copied him. It wasn't the force of the arms but of the whole skeleton moving forward and backward to lift the oars behind and lower them ahead. Without friction from the waves the boat moved by itself beneath our feet. "*Cuóncio, nun t'allenta*"—Slowly, don't wear yourself out, he told me.

· · ·

I rowed for two hours in the still waters of the night. The sound of the oars was two syllables, the first accented when they went into the water, the second longer until they came out. *An-na, an-na,* between the two syllables a woman's name was pronounced on our breath. After two hours he took over the oars and I slowly lowered into the sea the line with the hundred baits. When we were done the day was beginning.

All around us on the surface of the sea, a shiver passed, anchovies threatened by the tuna billowed up and leaped out, the water rippled from the swarm in flight. We were in the middle, the fisherman grabbed the net and lowered it at random amid the mass. He hauled up a living handful that he flipped into a bucket. It was robbery.

The sun appeared, dragging its feet, the sound of gas catching fire, the burner lit, and on it he set a coffeepot, dented and charred. He wet his head and put his beret back on, I made the same gesture. The coffee whistled air through the beak like a rooster. He lifted his cup to the sky to greet the rising day. We drank inhaling its smell of earth on the sea, one mile from the shore.

· · ·

Following his pointers I aimed for the sandbank, a field in the middle of the sea that could be located through a couple of finders: the whole outline of the Sant'Angelo promontory would appear and Vivara Island was supposed to look like a laurel leaf. In that strait of the sea you rested on the sandbar. The sun was already giving off a sweaty-faced glare. Give us today our azure bread attached to the bait hook. In its slow movements there was prayer, not pretense. The sea, at our bidding, let itself be gathered. We lowered the line weighted with pieces of squid. First to rise from the bottom was the sparkling white of the ombrina, then the red rockfish, flapping wildly. Under the beating sun the sea began to shift, slow waves pushed the boat off course. We corrected the drift with the oars. It was the hour of waiting before hauling in the line dangling from the two floats. We went to retrieve them. With slow, regular strokes, he coiled the line back in the baskets. After fifty meters an eel slithered aboard. He picked it up with a net, removed the swallowed bait from its mouth, and threw it in a tub. It was followed by a small grouper, a medium-sized one, and the glorious sea bream, pride of any man on his way back from fishing.

. . .

A couple of times the line went taut, stuck to some spot on the bottom. He ordered me to row in one direction, guessing the angle from which to free it. We finished and took turns at the oars. We went in the direction of the current, each stroke was supported by a push from the stern. We arrived at the beach of our departure as the bells were calling the noonday mass. He offered me the small grouper and shook my hand. It was bleeding because of my lack of practice with the oars. We had exchanged ten words at the right moments.

On the return ferry I stretched out to sleep on the wooden seats smelling of varnish and salt. A sailor woke me, we had arrived. It was already city around me, I hadn't heard it approach. For a little while I was dazed, not knowing where I should go, what to do. The burning in my hands revived me.

That night Don Gaetano cooked with tomato the best grouper in the world, picked clean all the way down to the bone.

It was summer and the swelling in my pants often returned to me. Don Gaetano taught me a few simple electrical and plumbing jobs, and sent me to take his place on a few repairs. I would pick up tips. One afternoon when the usual call from the widow came he told me to go up. I appeared with the toolbox, she let me in. Even at home she wore the little hat with the black veil. The blinds were closed, the room cool and dusky. She showed me the way to the bathroom to repair the drainpipe of the sink. I crouched down to unscrew the trap, she stayed close by, her naked knees at eye level. While I forced the nut with the monkey wrench, her knees started to bump against me in little thrusts. Saliva filled my mouth. Her hand went to my hair to ruffle it, I stopped working, stayed still. She squeezed and started to pull on my hair. I let go of the monkey wrench, I obeyed her. She turned off the light and pressed her belly against mine. Her arms climbed to my neck and squeezed it, pushing it slowly against her face. She opened my mouth with two fingers and then with her lips. I raised my hands in response, she took them and placed them behind her back. Then she started fumbling for my sex. My back was to the sink, she pressed against me and my sex entered her body. She moved me around. It was nicer than inside the cloud. She lifted my hands to her breasts and started to breathe out, faster and faster, until a push that took away all the blood in my body. A transfusion from her to me had happened. This must be the *facimm'ammore*, the let's make love, that men and women say to each other.

I was in a sweat, my underwear at my feet, my back stiff from withstanding her pushes without leaning against the sink. She broke away from me, turned on the lights, and washed between her legs. She told me to do the same. Then I picked up my tools. "If I need you I'll call you." "Yes, ma'am." And that was my first repair job.

. . .

The second time was already easier, no bathroom, straight to her bedroom, she undressed me, stretched me out on her bed, and climbed on top. The thrusts were hers. We stayed attached longer. Don Gaetano asked me if I was happy to do it, I said yes, with my head.

"She's replaced me with you."

I said that wasn't right.

"It's right and as it should be. She's young and I couldn't keep up with all her calls."

I could. She had a wild variety of fantasies, one was in total darkness. I had to hide, she came in looking for me. I stayed for an hour, then I went back downstairs. It lasted until the beginning of autumn, I used to go in the afternoon. Then her mourning ended, she took off her veil and left the house wearing colors. The calls came to an end. It was Don Gaetano who had recommended me, he told her I was trustworthy, a kid who didn't talk.

"You needed a little nature. Now that you've known it, an encounter with the girl from the third floor might even happen to you."

"And how will I recognize her? Ten years have passed, a lot of time."

"*Guaglio'*, time is not a lot, it's more like a forest. If you have known the leaf, you recognize the tree. If you looked into her eyes, you will find her again. Even if a forest of time has gone by."

. . .

I practiced doing repairs. I learned quickly, once I saw something done I repeated it correctly. I made some money. I understood the channels, the wires, that carried the flows that had to be enclosed in the ducts, to run between the poles and the switches. I liked being the stationmaster of the circuits. Controlling water, electricity, was a game for me. It wasn't much of a game when the soil stack got clogged and had to be emptied of excrement. The first time I gagged. Don Gaetano had me tie a handkerchief around my mouth and nose.

The autumn of the last year of school had begun. At night I studied and the afternoon I spent at the loge for the card game and to fill in for Don Gaetano. One afternoon that we weren't needed for any chores, a drizzle was falling from low clouds, coming down soft and sticky. We were playing a hand of scopa, my back was to the window, Don Gaetano got up to answer someone who had appeared at the door. I took advantage of the interruption to go to the bathroom. I came back and sitting at the table were two girls in raincoats. One of them was looking around, the other wasn't. One was blond, self-confident, talking with Don Gaetano, the other wasn't. I remained off to the side.

. . .

The blonde asked whether there were any unrented apartments in the building. Don Gaetano took his time to get a sense of the person he was dealing with, asked whether they would like a coffee. They said yes and took off their raincoats. He put the pot on the fire. Out of habit I avoid looking the girls in the face. Otherwise I get embarrassed.

"Here we don't post rent signs, we spread the word. Right now there's nothing, but a three-room apartment on the third floor is supposed to open up."

Don Gaetano paused. He was at the burner, standing, and out of the corner of his eye he was staring at the one who had still said nothing. I could see her brown hair, sugared-chestnut-colored, held back behind her neck by a hairpin. "The apartment where you lived when you were a little girl," said Don Gaetano with a half smile at the silent one. I took a step backward and bumped into the coffeepot, which didn't want to fall.

"Anna," came out of my mouth. The blonde covered my voice by asking whether they could visit the apartment. Anna turned around very slowly and looked at me, eyes wide and still, as if on the other side of a window. "*Guaglio'*, mind the coffee, it's boiling." I twisted around and turned the coffeepot upside down, removing it from the flame.

"Go upstairs to ask whether the young ladies can see the apartment." I went out like a sleepwalker, my mouth half-open. As I climbed the stairs I traveled to the past, the times I had risked waiting in front of that door to hear a noise, in the hope of seeing her come out. It never happened. And now here I was about to knock on her door to bring her back here. The past was a staircase and I was climbing back up.

. . .

I returned and there were four cups, one for me, too. "If you accompany them, Don Gaetano, the young ladies can go up." I drank the coffee without being able to look up. The window that separated the little girl from the world had fallen, the shards must be on the ground. They went upstairs to the apartment, I washed the cups, then I left the loge and went into the courtyard so I could be in the rain. I had dived across the wet pavement many times to steal the ball from feet, from kicks. I looked at the rain pipe going straight up, passing next to the first-floor balcony. Now it was inhabited by flowerpots with the last basil of the year.

I leaned my head back till I could see the third floor. She was there, behind the windows, and she was looking down. I lowered my eyes, the coffee climbed back up inside my throat, pushed by the beat of a hiccup from my diaphragm. I returned to the loge, to the bathroom, and I threw up.

. . .

They came downstairs, the blonde asked Don Gaetano to notify her when the lease expired, they were ready to take it over. Anna followed, looking around. I helped them to put on their raincoats, the blonde tossed her hair outside her collar, a gesture that forced me to pull my head back to avoid getting it in my face. Anna kept hers under her collar, divided by a line that parted it in two. A smell of rain rose to my nose, stolen from behind her. The weather had worn that smell to be recognized. She thanked me for my small bit of help, turned around and shook my hand, noticed the injury from rowing and smiled. That contact held the promise children make to see each other tomorrow. Then she shook Don Gaetano's hand. The blonde had already left and outside it had stopped raining.

"Are they coming here to live?"

"I don't think so, they only wanted to visit. The other girl brought along the blonde, who talks like a lawyer."

"I've wanted to see her for so long I forgot what she might look like. Waiting made me forget what I was waiting for. How can something so absurd be possible, Don Gaetano?"

"At the orphanage I waited to be old enough to go out, then the day came and I didn't remember what I had been waiting for."

"I never imagined she'd be so pretty. So bold, pensive, a little battered, someone arriving from a trip. Do you think she'll come back?"

"I don't think. I know."

. . .

We didn't play scopa, I had no head for it. We were distracted by a small commotion, a visit from the tax auditor. He had come to deliver an assessment, a summons, to La Capa, the cobbler, the same one who two years ago had picked four winning numbers in the Naples lottery. The auditor was a government official, quite smug about his job, and he had a northern accent. But getting La Capa to understand something in Italian was beyond his reach. I go to call the cobbler and tell him he has a visitor at the loge. He comes by and then begins the following exchange, which I immediately copy down in my notebook.

"Are you Mr. La Capa?"

"At your service, Excellency."

"I am here to serve you with a citation."

The cobbler made a worried face, told him to have a seat, that he would bring him a glass of water.

"I'm sorry to have been the cause of any agitation," all the while forcing him into the chair.

"Agitation? What are you talking about, Mr. La Capa, I have here a citation."

The cobbler had decided the man was agitated. He placed a glass of water in his hand.

"But I'm not thirsty, Mr. La Capa, let's not waste time, I am here on behalf of the Ministry of Finance."

"Congratulations, and who is the lucky girl? Your fiancée?"

"No one. I am here about your tax liability."

"So, you're a liar, are you?"

"How dare you!"

The poor auditor was audibly irritated but also intimidated because La Capa had two hands on him that were one size short of a shovel, and they were attached to two arms that were larger than life.

"You see, you're agitated."

The other man started to stand and La Capa sat him back down with a light tap that glued him to the seat.

Don Gaetano was surveying the scene, unperturbed. The cobbler wanted to explain himself.

"Listen here, Mr. Liar from the tax liability: *chillo ca cuntrolla 'e bigliett d'o tram se chiamma cuntrollore*—the guy who inspects streetcar tickets is the ticket inspector, right? And you are from liability, which makes you a liar."

"Listen here, Mr. La Capa, this is an outrage."

"*Ma quanno mai, qua nisciuno s'arraggia*—No one is raging out here. But you look too pale, like an undertaker, *chillo d'e ppompe funebri*, doesn't he, Don Gaetano? He's wearing black shoes, the kind that chase funerals."

"Now you're really going overboard." The poor auditor tried to stand up, but La Capa returned him to the chair with a blow of the sort that nails a sole to a shoe. The auditor realized that things were taking a turn for the worse and started glancing around for assistance. Don Gaetano was an Egyptian sphinx.

"My good man, do you or do you not understand that I am here to inspect your income?"

"No, you show me no respect, and you may not come in."

"My dear Mr. La Capa, are you hard of hearing?"

"Hard of hearing? Me? Why I can hear what the flies are saying all the way down in Piazza Municipio. You're the one that talks foreign."

"I speak Italian, as is only normal."

"Oh no you don't, with my Norma you could only speak Neapolitan."

The auditor felt lost, ran a hand through his thinning hair, and shut his mouth, giving up any effort to stand up.

"*Bevete 'o bicchiere*"—Drink up, La Capa ordered.

He obeyed with his eyes closed. Before he could start crying Don Gaetano finally stepped in.

"I'll take care of the auditor, go on back to your apartment now, La Capa."

"Good idea, you handle him, *io nun aggio capito niente 'e chistu furastiero*—I don't understand a word this foreigner says."

Don Gaetano accepted the summons and released the auditor.

"We're never going to see him around here again."

"Don Gaetano, if you had waited another minute, we would have had to take him to the hospital."

"He deserved to meet La Capa. For once in his life a poor guy has a stroke of luck, right away the state comes by and wants to take it away. La Capa was right, that guy was wearing black shoes for a funeral."

· · ·

The rest of the afternoon Don Gaetano taught me how to wrap hemp around threaded pipes, to smear grease to seal the joint between two pipes. I still hadn't used the threader, the tool that cuts the pipes and threads them. He let me try it a couple of times, I succeeded.

"I have to redo an installation, I'm going tomorrow. If you give me a hand we'll be done by noon and split it down the middle."

"Down the middle? I can't. You're the master, I'm the assistant. Give me a tenth and we're good."

"I'll give you a fourth and not another word."

And so it went. The following Sunday from seven in the morning until twelve o'clock sharp we redid the installation. I was back home at two o'clock and in front of the locked door Anna came toward me. Don Gaetano had insisted on my washing my face and hands, I could shake hands without getting her dirty. "Can you let me in?" She was in a bit of a rush and looking around. I opened the door without shaking, but my throat was choking. I couldn't take her to the room where I slept, there wasn't enough space for two. I went into the loge. In those few rooms there was a door I had never opened and I knew it led to a downward staircase. I opened the door, it had to lead to the hiding place. My breath came out, inviting me to follow it. I lit a candle and headed down. Anna placed a hand on my back, but heavily, I felt a pressure from it that put me off balance. The silence of the tufo opened and closed around our footsteps.

. . .

We arrived in the storeroom I had entered ten years earlier. I rested the candle on a shelf higher up, we stood still. The candle cast ribbons of flame on her hair, her face. Her eyes responded to the light with sparks. Her breath was calm, it didn't shift the air. I hadn't been down there since then, I told her.

"Everything in this building is smaller than I remember as a child, except you."

Her voice crossed the ages. It started out childish and ended up adult. When she got to the "you," she touched me. Then her hand raised my arm to her shoulder. My other arm went around her hip by itself: a figure from the start of a dance.

"Here we are, this is how I imagined it. You climbed the balcony to see me, I descended the stairs to meet you halfway. You had a secret in a tower where we would dance. The desires of children command the future. The future is a servant who's slow, but faithful."

Anna spoke without a sliver of accent, a language of books. Her breath cherished each line. She stopped as if to start a new paragraph. It was my turn.

"I waited for you until I forgot why. What remained was an expectation in my awakenings, leaping from bed to greet the day. I open the door not to go out but to let the day in."

I leaned my temple against hers.

"Anna, it's been an eternity."

"It's over. Now begins time, which only lasts a few moments."

"Every day I used to hope that the ball would land on the closed-off balcony. I climbed it with the support of your looking at me. And then from the terrace, after I threw the ball down to get their eyes off me,

I had to reach your face in the windows. We should have gotten married then, as children. How did you recognize me?"

She moved her head away, looked at me by the profile of the candle.

"I need to kiss to respond."

With my dry lips I went toward her smooth, slightly parted lips. First my nose inhaled a liter of drunken oxygen, then Anna's breath entered mine. When holding its breath the body races to the lips for the most perfect bond.

"Do you feel the same thing, too, a wax sealing the edges of a letter?"

I sensed Anna's words in my nose. They did not pass from her voice or to my ears. Can you hear thoughts with the nose? And you, Anna, can you hear mine? The reply was her lips, which broke away and said yes.

. . .

Nothing more happened with our bodies. The climax of our lips, the breath swallowed by the nose, mixed with thoughts, was enough for us. We had fulfilled the childhood desire, the dance in the dungeon and the kiss. The exhaustion of the final stretch overcame us. We sat down on the cot, next to each other, illuminated by the burning light of the flame. I stood up to bring it lower, setting it on the ground, and sat down again.

"I am not by your side, Anna, I am your side."

"You are the missing part returning from abroad to rejoin."

The light rose from our feet and spread warmth over our faces.

"It's not a candle, it's a forest in flames," I said.

Anna took my hand and placed it in her lap.

"We don't have time, it's expired, we're stealing another extension."

"So shall I exchange the end for the beginning, the first kiss for the last?"

"Kisses are not for counting, my side, this was not the first kiss but maybe the thousandth of the kisses I awaited. No kiss is ever the first, they are all the second. The first I gave you from behind the windows the day of your climb to the balcony. For me you were climbing the cliff. It was then I granted you my first time."

Her hand squeezed my fingers, where my blisters still stung.

"And this is another second kiss because the hands also kiss and embrace."

"Your eyelids are curved like the keel of a boat, Anna."

"I have eyelids that do not sleep and do not weep."

. . .

What separates us, what age is about to end? The thought finds its answer.

"The thief I'm engaged to will be getting out of prison soon. He wants to marry me and leave for South America."

"I have no right to know. If I could, I'd ask why I didn't see you outside the windows."

Anna replied by breaking away, her hands on her knees.

"I was a closed girl, closed from inside myself. Unable to cry even after a beating. Today someone like that is called autistic. I'm crazy, my side, a girl who gives orders to dreams and desires. I am the queen of witches' blood, of the women burned at the stake. Do you see how this candle desires me? They brought me away from here, to a clinic on the hills. I never saw my parents again. I inherited from them. At eighteen I left the clinic and came back here. I didn't remember where the building was. I'm living in a hotel.

For a year I've been looking for this place and for the window. I wanted to remember what I had seen. And instead I remembered what I'd never heard, my name uttered by you. My name uttered by a boy who was making coffee in a loge, a sound I remembered without ever having heard it before. I'm made of leaves like a tree and I recognize a wind even if it has never blown. After that it was easy to look out from behind the windows and rediscover you there. It was you, a little tree all grown in the spot where it had been left. You are made of wood, too, to burn and to navigate."

A shiver ran through me before the candle.

"Are you afraid? Yes, tremble, my side, your shiver is just a down payment. Tremble all you want, here in the dungeon you can tremble safely."

She gave a cool caress to my burning forehead. Her gesture took away my fear, a cloth removing the dust.

The candle wick was shedding sparks. Anna picked one up and brought it to her tongue.

"What do you think, do the stars taste more like sugarloaf or salt?"

"I don't know, I've never tasted them."

"I have, I spent many nights on the balcony of the house of the enclosed children. In the summer the stars shed crumbs that fall in your mouth."

"And what are they like?"

"Salty, the flavor of bitter almond."

"I used to prefer them sweet."

"No, there'd be so many the soil would be destroyed. Some nights there were storms of crumbling stars. The earth is seeded with them, it receives without being able to give back. So from below the prayers rise up to be forgiven of debt, from trees and animals that give thanks."

"Do you pray, Anna?"

"No."

"Why not?"

"Because I come from there, from a seed that traveled in the icy tail of a comet."

"And you came to be born here, amid the narrowest and loudest alleyways in the world?"

"Yes, the lost train of the comet ends up in the mouth of volcanoes. My seed fell into the crater. The eruption of 1944 spat it out. The matter from which I was made breathes in the tufo of this dungeon."

"I am also a child of the volcanic rock of this place, Anna. I don't come from space, like you, but from the enclosure of a courtyard. I used to lift my eyes not to the heavens but to your window, which was the step of heaven descended to earth. My breath rose to your windows and formed a mist over them. You dried it with your sleeve. I love the glass of windows. I could see the elbows that held your head. The glass windows on the courtyard carried the reflection of your figure all the way down to my room. They were a relay team, if one was missing your figure was lost in the air. I thank the glass of the courtyard. And what am I supposed to do with happiness now that you've come down from the windows? What can I do, Anna?"

She was shaken.

"Do? What a strange thought, you think there is 'to do' between us? Here there are no verbs, just our names, nothing to add. Here there is a bed on which we neither lay nor embraced, dry as an altar before the sacrifice."

"Do you want to lie down?"

"Not now, my side, this bed is a wound, it should be covered with bandages. I will bring sheets." She stood up and so did I. She held my hand and took a step toward the stairway. I picked up the candle and followed her. In place of my feet was a swallow's tail, beating from happiness to go out into the open air. I accompanied her to the main door. It was solid and needed a push from the shoulders. I didn't have the strength to open it and separate us. She opened it with a single arm, effortlessly. From her slight body came a violent burst of compressed energy. The door swung open like a curtain. My face was struck by the noise of hinges and the breath of Anna, already turning away: "See you Sunday."

. . .

I remained behind the closed door. The child had been fulfilled. Of all the things I had missed I focused on the most fantastic one, Anna's kiss. I didn't miss what belonged to childhood, a family. I had done without, like so many in the postwar years. No melancholy but rather the freedom to set the time for my days without a clock. I had my room, the school, the courtyard. I had the soup brought over by the maid of my foster mother. She had saved me from the orphanage to which I was destined. Out of that whole childhood, the missing thing I chose was the girl in the window. When she disappeared, life shrank to little cages. I had to live without the freedom of lifting my eyes. Ten years later Anna had descended from the third floor all the way down to the dungeon for our childhood wedding. Time was a letter and had been sealed with a kiss.

Anna was crazy, what did this mean? Don Gaetano arrived while I was still in a daze behind the main door. I told him right away I had misused the loge and even opened the door to the descending stairs. I had no other place to take Anna.

"You did the right thing, *guaglio'*, forget about it."

"Don Gaetano, did you know Anna was crazy?"

"They treated her like she was. She didn't want to speak, she didn't want contact with anyone. They sent her to a clinic, they were ashamed of her. The whole time she was here she never went out."

"She's the one who says she's crazy."

"Crazy people don't know it and they don't say it."

"What do you mean?"

We had entered the loge and Don Gaetano started slicing vegetables.

"In the age of commotion it's not enough to have heart to withstand the surge of the blood. The surrounding world is small next to the grandeur that fills the chest. It's the age in which a woman has to shrink to the small size of the world. An impulse inside her makes her think she won't manage, it takes too much violence to diminish herself.

"It's the age of risk. Women have a physical exaltation that we can never know. We can be exalted by a woman, they are exalted because of the force inside them. It is the ancient energy of the holy priestesses who guarded the fire."

. . .

I helped him peel the potatoes. His words about Anna fit perfectly, but around her feet, no higher.

"What should I do?"

"Go lighter on the peeling, no part of the potato should be thrown away. It should be like the wood shaving lifted up by a planer."

"What should I do about Anna?"

"You have to see her, get to know her to be able to chase her from your thoughts. She's not for you. But you won't be free until you get to know her."

"I don't want to be free. With her I want to be locked inside a room."

We put the vegetables on to boil and played scopa. At the end of every hand the odd cards came back even. Scopa was a game that instilled peace.

With Anna the swelling in my pants hadn't happened. In the summer it had become swift, the widow enticed me down there. With Anna it hadn't happened. The kiss had brought blood to my lips, I had the smell in my mouth. Anna gave me a buzzing in my ears, a dry nose, burnt lips, thirst. During the day a burst of fever rose and fell. I had to drink water to keep from drying out.

· · ·

I studied at night as usual. I enjoyed Latin, a language devised by a puzzle master. To translate it was to seek a solution. I didn't like the accusative case, it had an ugly name. The dative was nice, the vocative theatrical, the ablative essential. Italian was lazy for leaving the cases behind. In history the three little wars of independence bored me, but I was intrigued by the resistance of the South, swept under the rug with the label "banditry." The victors need to denigrate the vanquished. The South had remained fond of its defeats. It was a much bloodier military epic than the Risorgimento skirmishes, like the bizarre twin battles of Custoza, lost twice over a distance of years. Cavour didn't appeal to me, Mazzini was the founder of an armed gang, Garibaldi had arrived at a lucky moment, Pisacane at the wrong one. History was a kitchen full of ingredients, change the measurements and a completely different dish comes out.

I couldn't play the same game with chemistry and physics. The atoms had divided up the world

peacefully, but there had been an era of war between oxygen and hydrogen before reaching concord
through the formula of water. Water is a peace treaty.
Chemistry was the study of the balance achieved by
earthly matter.

. . .

I didn't have much to do with my classmates. I lent
a hand during tests, but without the urge to speak to
them or the teachers. I answered and left it at that.
Saturday afternoons I was summoned for the soccer
game.

The goalie is a point of view. He has to predict and
be ready for the shot from his station. When forced by
a play in the penalty box, he has to dive into a thicket
of feet, paying dearly for the advantage of using his
hands. I had the secondary advantage of not giving
a damn about myself. They assigned me the noblest
position, defense, and I honored it. To allow a goal
was to fail. There are no unblockable shots. There
are errors of position in predicting the shot. I blocked
penalty kicks, but not the ones kicked by the left foot,
lefties are less predictable. In their foot they have an
instinct that depends not on the brain but on the foot.
I'm a leftie, too.

Between school and soccer my relations were a free throw. I threw the ball and questions back into play. I was a little autistic myself, without Anna's extremism. She was made to stay inside a fortress and repel sieges.

• • •

I kept losing at scopa, zero for three. Even if I was dealt a lucky hand and was holding the trump card, took all four sevens, Don Gaetano would still end up compensating by playing the cards he'd seen. He didn't read my mind, he didn't exploit his advantage, he calculated the probabilities.

"Don Gaetano, when will you pay me the honor of a game of scopa?"

The count made an appearance at the loge and invited himself to our table.

"You're lousy at scopa, no offense. Play with the *guaglione* and if you win we can play a game."

The count was happy to play a qualifying round with me, the first to score eleven, and he lost.

"The cards don't like me," "What a spiteful game," "I can't do a sweep when he's got the cards." He became irritated and left, saying good-bye only to Don Gaetano.

His aftershave made me sneeze. When the count left, Don Gaetano opened the window and chased the air out, fanning it with a dish towel. "Living inside that cloud of cologne turns him into an idiot, no wonder he loses at scopa."

. . .

Don Gaetano was humming a song he had learned on the ship that took him to Argentina.

> *Me ne vogl'i' lontano tanto tanto*
> *che nun m'ha da truva' manco lo viento*
> *che nun m'ha da truva' manco lo viento*
> *manco lo sole che cammina tanto.*

> I want to go far far away
> where not even the wind can find me
> where not even the wind can find me
> or even the sun who travels all day.

It was the nursery rhyme of a young peasant from the Marches region who occupied the neighboring bunk in the hold. What he remembered from his twenty years in Argentina was the voyage, the ocean. It was the wish fulfilled of the little boy who had climbed over the gates of the orphanage to see the ships lit up at anchor in the bay.

"Voyages are the ones you take by sea, on ships, not on trains. The horizon has to be empty and divide the sky from the water. Nothing should be around and immensity should bear down from above. Then it's a voyage. Despite the misery that had driven them, some were weeping, loss was gnawing at them. Except for the few and the worst, no one had a spirit of adventure. The money for the ticket had been collected from the savings of different families, their investment in the future, which would be repaid by their relative's success. The crushing duty, the obligation to find fortune, was as daunting as the vastness of the sea. To those who were weeping I used to say their salt water was making the ocean even wider. The voyage was supposed to help forget the point of departure. It lasted almost a month and at the end the men disembarked ready, their noses to the air."

. . .

That Saturday I broke my nose. I dived between feet to grab the ball, I was early but in the heat of the run the other guy kicked anyway and caught me in the face. I didn't let go, the referee called a foul, bringing my hand to my nose I found it had shifted. I must have been a sight, the other guy looked at me in shock. A medical student took my nose between his fingers and straightened it with a sharp move. The cartilage had derailed and he put it back on track. He told me there was an indentation in the bone, an infraction. They put in another guy for me, I held ice to my nose to slow the loss of blood.

At the end of the game my adversary came over to apologize. I remembered a sentence from Don Gaetano's stories, I answered, "Some things happen the day before."

"The day before what?"

"The day before happiness."

He went on his way, shaking his head. I went home with my eyes swollen purple. Don Gaetano made me a compress of salt and water.

. . .

I slept aching all over in a swirl of dreams. When I woke it was dark. In my nose I felt nothing, a plug of dried blood was obstructing it. I didn't want to give up my nose before Anna. I wrapped a little toilet paper around the cartridge of a ballpoint pen and used it to open a passage in my nostrils. The pain squeezed teardrops from me. I tried to dissolve the clot with warm water, it came out rose-colored. Is this what they meant by rose water?

I tricked the pain with thoughts of Anna, I exhaled through my nostrils but it came out in my throat. The pushing and rinsing made the plug give way all at once and I started bleeding again. The smells could rise, the smell of sugared chestnuts, that's what I had wanted to achieve. The rest of the day I rinsed my nostrils in warm water to prevent clotting.

"Don Gaetano, I'm a chimney sweep."

"Leave that poor nose of yours alone."

I insisted on doing the job we had planned. "My face is bruised, not my arms." It was an easy job, a new electrical setup, wires to be passed through cable ducts and connected on the other end. We were finished at noon. The soup fumes surprised me, they smelled like blood. I chewed on some bread with olives. Don Gaetano insisted on my drinking a glass of wine. "For the blood you've lost, wine evens the score."

Yes, it did. At the tavern, instead, wine went beyond evening the score and sent it into a spin. Don Gaetano used to go there at night for a little company. And on his way home he would be holding up by the arm a guy overtaken by wine.

"Last night the man leaning against me must have vomited a liter on the streets. They drink without eating, with the pocket change they have they pay for wine without a piece of bread. He apologized to me. 'Think nothing of it,' I told him, 'I am the one who feels sorry for you, for being emptier now than you were before.' The tavern is better than the theater, every table is a comedy. No tragedies, at the tavern they only offer lighter fare, people with heavy problems keep away."

After eating he slipped his coat on and went out, saying he would be back late.

"When you've finished your business, lock up the loge and we'll see you tomorrow."

. . .

The silence behind him, after the closed door, the silence of a Sunday afternoon singed my ears. I placed the cold palms of my hands over them. I inhaled through my nose, there was a passageway but I rinsed it out with warm water anyway. The rose water came out again.

I didn't mind that I'd broken my nose the day before. When you are called to defend the goal you are responsible for the whole team. The day before freedom Don Gaetano had gone to fight together with the people of Naples. He hadn't shut himself indoors to wait. He had done the necessary thing and so would I.

And if freedom had found him dead the next day? It would have been worse to find him hiding. Freedom has to be earned and defended. Not happiness, which is a gift, it doesn't matter whether you're a good goalie and block the penalty kicks. Happiness: how dare I name it without knowing it? It sounded shameless in my mouth, like when someone boasts of knowing a celebrity and calls him by his first name, saying Marcello, to mean Mastroianni.

. . .

All I knew about Anna and happiness was that—the name. If she didn't come, where would I look for her? I shouldn't have allowed myself certain familiarities. After she's arrived I'll be able to tell her what it is, this famous happiness.

I took my hands off my ears. They had heated up my thoughts. The silence was gone. From one balcony came the voice of a radio, from another the clatter of dishes. I was supposed to wash them and I did, then I went out to the courtyard. Above me the clouds were moving upward. The pavement was wet from dripping clothes. The wind had appeared and I was stung by the melancholy of the fading day. I imagined the sunset, the sun descending to earth behind a hill, dragging the enchained clouds along behind it. I went out into the street, I didn't have a timetable to wait for Anna. Only a remnant was left of the whole day of happiness.

If she didn't come what should I call this day? I shouldn't call it at all. It would be an ordinary day, with all the necessary things inside, including a little Greek homework. But I didn't care for Plato, he had gotten it into his head to write down the dialogues of Socrates: how dare he? Did he take notes in the evening as I do with Don Gaetano's stories, or did he memorize them? Plato cheated, he put whatever he felt like into the mouth of his teacher and the others. He hid himself behind them. Is that any way for a writer to behave? No, it isn't. A writer has to be smaller than the subject he is describing. You have to sense the story running away from him every which way, and him capturing only a part of it. Anyone who reads has a taste for the abundance that overflows past the writer. With Plato instead the story is locked inside his enclosure, he doesn't let even a spurt of independent life escape. His dialogue is lined up in two rows, question and answer, then forward march.

. . .

The thought came to me watching the boys in uniform leaving the Nunziatella military academy two by two. When they were of high-school age like me they studied at the military school. Countering their descent to Santa Lucia came the upward current of Anna's elastic stride. She went uphill, head held high, a flowing dress wrapped tightly around her, tin foil around a bouquet. She was holding a parcel in her arms, her freshly washed hair followed the wave of her steps. I breathed through my nose to anticipate her smell from the distance. It was early evening, headlights had been turned on. They still couldn't illuminate, their purpose was to bring out a smile of reply from her. For an autumn evening she was dressed lightly. She wore shoes with heels that pushed her whole body upward. She had given color to her face.

"Let me in," and she cast a glance behind herself.

We entered quietly, through the main door, into the loge. Violent pulsations beat through my head, the pain in my nose was the tolling of bells. In the kitchen she turned around to give me the parcel, it was bed linen. She took my face between her hands and pushed her mouth retouched with red against mine, breathing deeply. It was an exquisite pain, a sharp pain in the eyes and melting chocolate in the mouth. At that point she noticed how swollen my face was around the nose. "What did you do?" "A kick, yesterday." She asked nothing more.

"I brought the sheets," and she headed toward the door leading to the staircase. I lit the candle and closed the city behind us.

· · ·

We went downstairs where no one would reach us. Anna followed, resting a hand on my neck. A force came from her body that moved the air.

The kiss was violent, the grip on my neck squeezed me. At the bottom of the steps, I set the candle down on the ground, she took care of the bed. I watched her moving. Rather than acting, she gave orders to things and they carried them out. She unrolled the first sheet in the air and it spread out over the mattress immediately and only had to be tucked in. The same with the second one and the blanket. She came close and started to undress me. My jacket was already off, the buttons of my shirt opened by themselves under her touch, she slipped it off me with a swift move that set both me and the flame swaying. She placed her ear on my taut chest, hollowed to the ribs, she squeezed my hips with her hands, I couldn't breathe.

"Slow down, Anna, you're crushing me."

"Quiet, I'm listening to your blood fill with oxygen."

She slipped off my belt, I was so skinny my pants fell by themselves. She pushed me to the bed and removed my shoes and socks. I was naked and I slipped between the sheets, she didn't even take off her shoes as she got into the bed.

I was between her and the wall. She lay on top of me. Her small breasts spread over my chest, her arms closed around my shoulders, blocking me. She wasn't applying pressure but I couldn't move. Even my legs were squeezed between hers. I could breathe, but not if she squeezed. I couldn't imagine so much effortless strength. Is this how women are in happiness? Can they crush in their embrace? The widow didn't act this way, I was the one who held her.

Anna buried her face between my shoulder and my neck, she rubbed her lips and her teeth, heat passed from her to me, moist, scorching. In my nose I smelled blood mixed with the cinnamon of her sugared-chestnut hair. The more she burrowed into my neck the more I surrendered. I had stopped noticing that I wasn't breathing. My sex swelled. I craned my neck to make more room for her inside me. For a time I could not measure, she was the rambler that wraps around a balcony. Our organs were separated by her dress and molded to each other. Hers loosened, she squeezed me in her arms, they creaked, she exhaled in short little grunts until a bite that called away the pain from my nose and made it run to my neck. Then she licked me there.

"Did I hurt you?"

"No."

"Are you afraid?"

"Yes."

"Of me?"

"Yes, and no courage will ever feel as good as this fear."

Anna lifted her head from my neck, her mouth was smeared with red. The candlelight colored her forehead with sunset. The locks of her hair were long clouds dragged along. She looked at me with eyes wide open, bent down with her lips of blood to mine. She pushed her mouth so deep inside mine I felt it in my throat. My sex was a block of wood glued to her womb. She eased up on her kiss, broke away, turned me around with a shift of her hips and I was on top of her. She loosed her arms from my shoulders, guided my hands to her breasts. She spread her legs, pulled up her dress, and holding my hips high pushed my sex against the opening of hers. I was something belonging to her that she controlled. Our organs ready, motionless in expectation, they barely leaned against each other, dancers on point. We stayed in that position. Anna looked down at them. She pressed on my hips, an order that thrust me inside. I entered. Not only my sex but me, I entered inside of her, into her depths, into her darkness, my eyes wide open without seeing a thing. My whole body had descended into sex. I entered to the rhythm of her thrusts and held still. While I was adjusting to the stillness, to the pulsing of blood between my ears and my nose, she pushed me a little out and then in again. She did it again and again, she held me forcefully and moved me back and forth to the rhythm of the undertow. Under my hands she shook her breasts, increased her thrusts. I entered as far as my groin and exited almost entirely, my body was one of her gears. She wasn't breathing, her gaping eyes saw far.

"Anna," I called from under her enchanted maneuvers.

"Yes, yes," were the perfect syllables that came from her lips. I called to her to make her breathe, I called to her to hear "yes." Her yes called to me and I too was about to say it when a thrust came that plunged me inside her with no turning back. She detached her hands from my hips and from my sex came all the yeses that had run inside her. My yes of emptying and farewell, of welcome, the yes of the marionette that goes limp without a hand to hold the strings. I slid onto my side and saw the bed stained with blood.

"It's ours, it is the ink of our pact. You placed inside me your initial, which I awaited intact. I will give it a body and a name."

"Anna, in your hands I know my purpose, this is why I was made."

She kissed the tip of my lips, passed her tongue over them.

"You have a good flavor, I had to restrain myself from eating you." She wasn't smiling.

"Can I kiss you now?"

"No, you are pollen, you must obey me, I am the wind."

. . .

Is this what happiness is, letting yourself be seized? Anna got up and lay on top of me.

With her legs she locked my arms, holding them still. With her right hand she closed her fingers over

my throat, with her left she caressed my face. She
started to squeeze.

"Do you want to die for me? Do want to die for
Anna the mad?"

Pinned beneath her, I managed to nod yes with my
head. She continued to caress and to squeeze me.

"Do you want to die for me, beneath me?"

I could only answer yes with my eyes. I didn't
breathe and I didn't defend myself. She squeezed
harder, I closed my eyes and saw white.

I woke up in the dark, the candle out, Anna van-
ished. I looked blindly for my clothes, got dressed,
and crawled up the stairs. The electric lights were a
slap to my eyes, I saw the time, it was nine o'clock at
night. Don Gaetano wasn't back. I went to my room and
washed up. I was smeared all over with red. My nose
was a secondary pain, my throat burned at the squeeze
point. I took a gulp of water that I couldn't get down.

I swallowed it in spoonfuls. I lay down on the bed.
It had happened, the day of happiness, the most awful
day of my short life.

. . .

The following morning I missed school. I couldn't get
up. I stopped taking the inventory of the parts that

hurt, it was faster to count the unharmed ones. My nose was blocked again and I left it that way. I didn't want to smell things, I didn't want to feel.

Don Gaetano dropped by when he didn't see me come out. He put a handkerchief around my neck. He said that at noon he'd bring me something to eat.

"Don't bother, I'm coming, it's just weakness." It was the weakness that makes you curl up to regain strength. Among the used books of Don Raimondo, I had read one about mountain climbing. It talked about the exhaustion of the summit reached, the impulse to fall asleep on top when it is urgent instead to descend, to avoid being overtaken by darkness far from the tent. I, too, had to descend from the summit of happiness. I never imagined it would be so tumultuous. Anna had been a storm and I did not want it to stop. I did not want the return to calm. The last thing I needed was to be sheltered from her. She was gone, she had moved on to discharge her violent energy. The day after happiness I was a mountain climber swerving out of control on the descent.

· · ·

Was I crazy too or was this the ineffable name of love? When someone said it at the movies, the word was wasted. Yet actors specialized in saying it, they had studied at the academy, practiced in front of the mirror, performed before a jury and other audiences to say in the end: I love you.

But what was written on walls and on the bark of trees was better. It had a better chance to arrive. To say it instead was a lump that fell to your feet. To say it was to waste it. Until the previous scene love had appeared in disguise, behind a few embarrassed moves, a cramp of the facial muscles. No sooner is it declared than it is betrayed, denounced by the formula that is supposed to proclaim it. Every I love you at the movies is a fiasco. No one knew how to say it. It was even more impossible for me, illiterate in the sentiments, to get around the word "love." I was only ready to belong to Anna, a body at the service of one of her urgent moves. I didn't want to come down from the summit I had reached. I wanted to stay up there to flutter like a pennant.

This thought filled me with energy. I got up from the bed, opened a book, studied. At noon I went to Don Gaetano. He had put vegetables on to cook. "I put in ten." Outside the autumn was shaking the windows. "The southwest wind, it lasts three days. It won't let the ships depart. If you're already at sea you shake, if you're on an island you could care less."

The salt air arrived in the alleyways, the city was flavored by the sea. The waves leaped over the break-water formed by the rocks and swept the waterfront.

After lunch we went out to meet the virgin air, a stranger to land. The oxygen lashed the crest of the waves. Pushed about by the southwest wind, my nose came unblocked. The coats of people who wore them were flapping, anyone with a hat held onto it with one hand. We walked from the port to Mergellina. We barely spoke, the wind snatched away the words.

. . .

'*O vient*', the wind, is swifter and smarter in dialect. '*O vient*', I walked and repeated, as I had done with Anna's name the day before. In the bay an American aircraft carrier floated light gray, an empty road broken off at the bow and the stern. It didn't fit in with the rest of the bay and the ships at anchor, it didn't fit in with the volcanic bubbles or the coast that shot from the sea on whaleback. The bridge of the aircraft carrier was a desert road, opposite the crowded city.

. . .

With all the force it invested, the wind had the effect of a massage on me, after Anna. The sky was ruffled with battered clouds, suddenly a jet of light burst through, blinding the foam on the waves. The true color of the sea isn't blue, it's white. You had to beat it against the rocks to see it come out. From within, nature must be white, while we are red inside. The sea, the sky, and even fire have a hidden whiteness, which I had seen beneath the fingers of Anna squeezed around my throat.

In Mergellina we entered a cafe, Don Gaetano wanted to buy me a coffee. We had been walking into the wind for an hour, our faces were scoured, our ears numb. The boiling cup warmed the fingers, it was right for the senses gathered around the handle. Leaning against the balcony we sipped the coffee on the tip of our lips, two hornets hovering over a flower.

"She's not for you." I was confused by the buzzing of the cafe and of the coffee machine puffing out steam, I didn't understand what he was saying to me at first.

"That girl is not for you."

"You've already told me and yes, you're right." I set the cup down. "I'm not enough of a man for her. For now I serve her purpose. What purpose I don't know. But I want to serve some purpose. Anna has a force you can't withstand."

Don Gaetano looked out the window toward the sea.

"Broken noses can be fixed but blood doesn't come back. What goes out is lost."

"What am I supposed to do with my blood? What am I supposed to save it for? It's yours if you want it."

Don Gaetano turned toward the counter again and downed the last sip of coffee. "You can do what you want with your own blood, not with someone else's."

I didn't understand and I couldn't ask. Outside the wind was stripping the white off the sea and scattering it over the street. The throwing of rice at newlyweds.

. . .

We set out. On our return the wind was at our backs, grabbed us by the scruff, landed a few kicks. A bigger wave sprayed us and a fit of merriment seized me and sent me running a few steps. Don Gaetano adjusted his soggy beret on his head. We were alone, *'o vient'* had locked the city into its homes. I imagined it abandoned, the people having fled, leaving doors open and pots on the fire. I could enter any building, sit down in the chair of the bishop or mayor, live in the Palazzo Reale, climb aboard the ships. Even the Americans had disappeared, leaving the aircraft carrier empty in the middle of the bay. The thought made my nose itch. It lasted until I saw them coming toward us against the wind. They were running in a group, T-shirts, shorts, and sneakers. The two of us all bundled up and them half-naked: the city's inhabitants had disappeared, the Martians had landed. Don Gaetano and I looked at our feet to see if we were on the ground or in the air. For us to run was a serious verb.

We would start running to flee an earthquake, an air raid. To run without being chased was boiling water without pasta. They passed by us focused on their movements, panting into the wind.

"They can't be real, Don Gaetano, this is a hallucination caused by the hot coffee."

"No, they are real. They are the latest people invented by the world, the latecomers. They know how to make war and automobiles. They are a population of overgrown children. If you ask them where they are they answer: far from home. They exist. For them we are the ones who don't exist. They cross our paths, pass in front of us, and don't see us. They live here and don't even see the volcano. I read in the newspaper that an American sailor fell into the mouth of Vesuvius. No surprise, he didn't see it."

Having left the waterfront, our own crowd, unruly and packed together, reappeared in the alleys. The elderly moved about unsteadily, looking for something to lean on, the children opened their arms to be carried by the bursts of wind. There were no clothes on the line, pulled in so as not to lose them to the gusts. Without sheets hanging you could see the sky above, patched with swollen clouds, smelling like fried panzarotti.

"Are you hungry?" asked Don Gaetano, casting an eye upward. He had heard my thought about the clouds. "It's their fault, they're fried masterfully."

It was the day of convalescence from happiness. Don Gaetano and *'o vient'* had taken it upon themselves to help me recover from Sunday. They were succeeding. This is how I learned about the happiness that is forgotten the day after. I wasn't thinking about Anna. The bruises on my body were enough to account for the oblique passage of happiness.

. . .

La Capa was at the loge, wanting to ask Don Gaetano for information.

"You that studied at the millenary."

"At the seminary."

"Like I was saying, you who studied there, did you know that in Rome they have cacatombs?"

La Capa's latest remark caught us off guard. I made a run for the bathroom, Don Gaetano felt the same urge but remained composed.

"I was there with my signora and the little girl, the *piccerella*. Many years ago there used to be the Christians who had to hide. But if you ask me, Don Gaetano, it's one thing to hide because you're Christian saints and mastiffs."

"Mastiffs?"

"You know, the ones masticated by the lions."

"Martyrs?"

"Yeah. Like I was saying, it's all well and good that your Christian saints and marbles."

"So now they're rocks? They're not marbles or even granite, they're martyrs."

"Whatever you say, but why did they have to go do caca in the tombs? I was there with my family!"

"Did it stink?"

"Not really. My signora, excuse me for saying this, but she's ignorant and didn't understand a thing, but me, *io me so' mmiso scuorno e vergognaria*—I was angry and embarrassed."

"They must have installed some kind of sanitary facilities."

"Of course, but why are they showing off a place like that, these Christian cacatombs."

"With all the beautiful things in Rome, why did you go there of all places?"

"They took us in the pulmonary."

"Was that the whole trip?"

"Nah, we went to St. Peter's and saw the whole columbarium."

"St. Peter's has columbaria?"

"Nah, there were rows and of columbaria, one nearby and the other, too."

"Colonnades?"

"Yeah. Like I was saying, they were so white and beautiful, like shoe cream. To make a long story short, I came down here to find out from you, wherever it is that you studied, at the millenary, if they told you there were cacatombs in Rome."

"This is the first I've heard of it."

And with that La Capa the cobbler went on his way, shaking his head, just back from his trip to Rome.

"Don Gaetano, you've got some stomach not to laugh in La Capa's face, you're a hero."

"Just the opposite, he terrifies me. If he realizes someone is making fun of him, he'll break his bones to smithereens. Be careful not to let a laugh escape in front of him, I wouldn't be able to defend you."

"That's why I hide as soon as he appears, but I listen to everything, I put a dishrag over my mouth and I listen."

. . .

We played scopa, finished the soup, I even drank a whole glass of Ischia wine. Don Gaetano was treating me differently, he hadn't called me *guaglio'* all day. After dinner he went back to telling stories about the war. "We had gotten used to hearing the fabrications of the radio, of the newspapers: the fatherland, the heroic defense of the borders, the empire. We had the empire: no bread, no coffee, but we had empire.

"When the Americans arrived the same radio and the same newspapers switched sides. From one day to the next the enemy had become the liberator. The same newspaper, articles signed by the same reporters, were writing the opposite. You had the impression you were reading in reverse. The Turks had become Christians, no one was nor ever had been Fascist. Their rule was to hold on to their spot. But there were so many changes this was a drop in the bucket.

White bread had arrived, the Americans distributed flour to the bakeries, there had been none for years. And together with the whiteness of the bread came the darkness of the Negroes, they had never been seen in the city. Elderly women on the street were forever making the sign of the cross."

Don Gaetano's stories opened my ears. His metallic voice pinched the nerves of the imagination. I could taste the bread of the first white flour baking, see the skyward eyes of the little old ladies baffled by the Negro soldier, feel between my fingers the printed paper of the new money that replaced the lira. Listening to Don Gaetano made me a secondary witness of his era. The story was a pied piper and my spellbound senses trailed behind it.

. . .

"In those days the city was freewheeling. Parties every night, hunger for life, to make up for lost time, to do business with the postwar. There were still bombings, this time by the Germans, lasting until spring, but we didn't pay them any mind, we didn't even go to the shelters when the sirens started up, which led to more losses. Before withdrawing the Germans had left time bombs in the city, one exploded at the central post office days later, a massacre. It was one of their tech-niques, I heard they did it in other places, too. They were sore losers.

"I guarded an abandoned arsenal that was still half full." All by himself, a real ace, guns in hand, had managed to commandeer it, preventing it from being plundered. "I guarded it day and night, I was holding the arms of the uprising. I made good money, but it was the easy money of the postwar, it was called am-lire. American liras. They were the ones who printed it, but the typographers in the city already knew how to make it better. It was money to spend, not to save."

"How did you end up becoming the doorman for this building?"

"It was your father."

Don Gaetano's answer came out of nowhere, so hard on the ears that my nose started bleeding. I brought my hands to my face to cover it and found it warm, wet. Don Gaetano led me to the sink to rinse myself with cold water. I couldn't look him in the face. My father: it was the first time I had heard him men-tioned, how was I supposed to know I even had one?

"Excuse me, Don Gaetano, I'm not feeling well, it would be better for me to go to sleep. Thank you for the day." The need to spend some time with my thoughts drove me away.

. . .

In bed I stuck my head under the covers. The wind was beating through the courtyard, a dog on a chain. So there had been a father for me, Don Gaetano had known him. Why hadn't I wanted to hear? Why did I feel like crying? At the third why I fell asleep. No dreams, I spent the nights in a submarine, where dreams do not descend. Dreams are fish of the surface. I woke up in time for school. I was bruised even where I had been all right the day before. My nose and capillaries were purple. I told Don Gaetano see you later, he said he would be expecting me at lunch.

At school my absence of the day before was justified by my face.

Visible wounds entitle you to respectability. I had gotten mine in the line of duty.

I started looking at adults from the strange possibility that one of them was my father. I didn't think of my mother, Don Gaetano hadn't mentioned her, so she continued not to exist. Until the day before my father had not existed, but no sooner had he been mentioned than he appeared in the faces on the street, at school. Many were odd, some were possible, I realized for the first time that I might resemble someone. I would clear up this story at lunch.

Somewhere in my head must have been the suspicion that Don Gaetano was my father. Now that I knew he was not, something was taken away from me without being replaced. Anna, the hiding place, the bed, were far away. If Don Gaetano had meant to clear them from my thoughts, he had succeeded. Now none of that happiness depended on me, nothing I could do would bring it back. If Anna returned she would find me ready, otherwise the happiness would expire. The nerve of expectation in my body did not tingle. So it's only impassioned when it doesn't know what to expect.

In those days I did not have a watch, the precious gift my peers received on their First Communion day. I had done that ceremony, too, but without parents I couldn't participate in the party and the reception. After church I went home. Without a watch I calculated time in city blocks. I only knew the time at school. There you didn't need a watch but everyone wore one. I didn't want one. I had no wants.

The oddest thing of all was the possessive: mine. Nothing was mine in this world, much less a father.

I was using the possessive for the first time. It wasn't worth much, it was needed to mention a father who had not been there.

That day in class I realized how many times the word "father" was said: of the homeland, of modern physics, of the church. A word resounded that had been inert until the day before. Until yesterday I had been nobody's child, an expression I liked after reading in the *Odyssey* that Nobody was the name of Ulysses in the cave of Polyphemus. Child of a false name, of nobody: I liked it. It excluded everybody. Now I was becoming the child of somebody, known to Don Gaetano, somebody from the city that at the right time had had a son and who knows whether he knew. Now somebody was cluttering my past. I had become his son. From a father you could go back to a grandfather and even further. The thought resembled the steps I had crawled up in the dark, after Anna.

The fathers I saw were awful. From them the children took slaps and kicks out of nowhere. Screams, blows, and sobbing came from the houses. None of that had happened to me. If an evening melancholy came over me when the mothers called to their children in the courtyard to come upstairs, I remembered the beatings that arrived all the way to my room and the score came out even. I plugged my ears, it wasn't enough. Children's screams of pain make it through anyway, they are conveyed from skin to skin.

There is one boy I can't forget. He was scrawny like me, even if he was two years older. His father wasn't ashamed to beat him even in the courtyard. The boy took the blows without a shout, without tears, but he made a move, a shudder of "no" with his head, a nervous twitch in his face that closed his eyes in resistance before us. I can't shake him from my sight. He stays with me, sainted by the bruises and blood from his mouth. He didn't defend himself and he didn't cry. He trembled in his futile heroism. He died under his father, who didn't even go to prison. Aniello, a diminutive for Gastano, a life diminished among the many that had ended early. I went to the funeral with Don Gaetano, his mother cried tearlessly for him. Aniello played goalie for the opposing team, we were the farthest apart, we exchanged glances. When his father found him in the courtyard playing and didn't want him to, he would grab him by the hair and start kicking him. Once I threw a rock at him. He didn't even notice. We weren't worth anything. If another rock had been thrown with better aim and force, if many of us had thrown, Aniello could have been saved. His face closed to avoid surrendering to tears under the blows, he brought tears to my eyes, wiped away with the back of my hand to pretend it was sweat. The game started up again, briefly silent, without Aniello.

· · ·

Don Gaetano had cooked pasta and potato soup, well rested, my favorite dish.

"I have to apologize for leaving like that last night."

People were walking past the loge, Don Gaetano greeted them and to be polite he would say: "*Fa-vo-ri-te*, would you like to try some?" Between one *favorite* and another, he informed me of the history that had preceded me. My father was a career soldier. He was forty years old when the war broke out. He married my mother, who was fifteen years younger, before leaving for Africa. He came home on leave just in time to find himself in plain clothes on armistice day, September 8, 1943, when Italy surrendered and the king ran away. My father went into hiding, then he took part in the uprising. He and Don Gaetano met in the days of battles in the city. My father had commandeered the German arsenal, by himself, in a standoff against the crowd that wanted to plunder it. He positioned himself in front, in uniform and with two pistols, one in each hand. The crowd went away, looking for an easier opportunity. Then he put Don Gaetano there to guard it. They became friends but were formal with each other.

· · ·

"The postwar was all hands on deck. The men threw themselves into making money and the women ran wild with the Americans.

"The women of Naples lost their heads and the rest. Every home hosted an American solider. They brought abundance, business, work. The girls went to their parties at Rest Camp. They had become more beautiful and more brazen. Not much public transportation circulated, the girls would ask the jeeps for a ride. They let themselves be picked up and they fell in love. There were crimes of jealousy. A husband found out that his wife was going with the Americans but he kept quiet, it was worth his while. Not just that, he would even accompany her. But once his wife said she enjoyed doing it with them and he went mad with jealousy. He killed her, his mother-in-law, his sister-in-law, and her husband, four at once, in Piedigrotta.

"Naples had been consumed by the tears of war, it let loose with the Americans, celebrated carnival every day. That's when I understood the city: monarchist and anarchist. It wanted a king but no government. It was a Spanish city. In Spain there has always been a monarchy but also the strongest anarchist movement. Naples is Spanish, it's in Italy by mistake."

. . .

"You had just been born when your mother fell in love with an American officer.

"Your father found out about it. He came to see me when I was already the doorman here.

"He had found me the job, in his building, after selling the rest of the German arsenal to the Americans. He came to me one morning and told me solemnly: 'Don Gaetano, you look after the child.' He went upstairs and shot your mother at home. That same night he boarded a boat to America and I heard nothing more about him. His name was . . ."

"Don't tell me, Don Gaetano, don't put in my head a name I can never remove. What use would it be, I can't carry it, I'm named after the woman who adopted me."

"In the early years I kept you with me."

"Why am I finding out this story today rather than yesterday or never?"

"Because you have to know. Yesterday you turned eighteen."

And now a birthday, another day that was good for others, like Christmas and Easter. But I know when Christmas and Easter arrive, it's written on the stores. I know that my birthday is in November. "When my mother died what day was it, do you remember?"

"No, not the day, it was spring, it was May."

. . .

I remained hovering over the pasta and potato soup. There was a place where she was in the ground. I imagined I should go with flowers. No. I'm a stranger, I don't even know her name if I have to ask. No, she is gone, too. They lived in this building, I don't want to know where. I came back from the wanderings of my thoughts.

"Don Gaetano, your pasta and potato soup has no rival."

"It's nice to see you've got an appetite, have some more, there's plenty. Help yourself."

The widow passed by in a white dress. She was about to speak to me, noticed my swollen face, and went to Don Gaetano, asking him to come up.

"At your service," he replied. He had lost hope.

"Do you mind clearing the table? Leave the dishes in the sink, I'll wash them later. And stay here in the loge till I get back."

"No need to worry."

· · ·

Child of: good-bye Nobody, good-bye false papers of Ulysses. They had trapped me between a murderous father and an unfaithful mother, between someone who had escaped overseas and another who had descended underground. I had no choice but to resemble them. I wasn't free to resemble nobody. The whole rest of the world was no longer there to be my origin. Was it because of my mother that I hadn't defended myself from Anna's grip around my throat? Was it her readiness to die for love? I cleared the table and brooded.

What had I taken from my father? Not jealousy. Over the widow who needed embraces or over an Anna who wasn't for me? I didn't have the military spirit either, the boys in the academy uniform to me were prison inmates.

I forced myself to imagine figures of jealousy: Anna writes to her boyfriend, she goes to visit him in prison, they embrace, who knows whether they can embrace in prison. Nothing, not a single nerve shifted. What reason did I have to be jealous? She had done the happiness thing with me while her boyfriend was locked up. He was the one who had the right to be jealous. Dear father, I don't take after you. I take after Don Gaetano, you were friends anyway. I take after Don Gaetano every day. He teaches me skills, he tells me history stories, for no reason, in your place. Dear father, they're knocking on the window, I'm going to go see what it is. When I come back don't be hanging around in my thoughts.

· · ·

I dried my hands, went to the window. Anna. "See you Sunday," she said, and disappeared. I was dumbfounded. I sat in Don Gaetano's chair to stare at the empty window. Climbing up my back was a shiver from my sacrum, which here they call the *osso pezzillo*, the tip bone, all the way up to my neck. A tenant passed by, asked for his mail, I gave him the wrong bundle, realized it, and chased up the stairs after him with the right one.

Then the greengrocer came by with a delivery for the lady on the top floor and called out from the courtyard as usual for her to lower the basket.

"*Signora Sanfelice, Calate 'o panaro. Signora Sanfelic-eee!*"

Turning to me: "*Nun ce sente cchiù, s'adda fa' n'apparecchio p'e rrecchie*"—She can't hear anymore, she needs to get an aid for her ears.

"A hearing aid," I tell him, for the sake of saying something and giving him someone to speak to.

"Yes, a jeering aid, Signora Sanfelic-eee!"

At his third shout the woman either heard or some-one knocked on her door to tell her to lower her basket.

"*Nu mumèe*"—Just a sec. What Signora Felice calls a sec is more like an hour. In her mouth the "sec-ond" starts off well but never ends. Don Gaetano says she has a trumpet of a voice that wakes the souls in purgatory.

"Lower the basket."

"Just a sec."

"Just a second," I add, to bring the word to an end.

"The basket," the greengrocer shouts hoarsely.

"Just a sec," you hear descending from the open window. The woman's voice has lost the "-ond" of the second, for now she only lowers the "sec-."

The greengrocer loses his patience and calls out again.

While waiting he says: "The lady can't find her bas-ket. Why doesn't she keep it by the window?"

Her neighbor in the apartment facing hers shouts at her to look under the sink.

A full-throated trombone of an answer: "*Nun ce staa*"—It's not there!

"Look behind the stove!"

"*Nun ce staa.* Concettina moved it. She straightens up and things disappear."

"Signora Sanfelic-eee!" The greengrocer starts up again with a choked voice he'd like to choke her with.

Right on time: "Just a sec."

"Just a second," from me.

Finally a cry of liberation fills the courtyard: "She's found it, she's found it."

"Thy will be done," a voice intones, shutting the window, followed by the closing of the other participating windows.

. . .

"See you Sunday": Had I seen her or was it a vision? What, am I getting visions now, of Saint Anna appearing to me? I've turned eighteen: now is not the time to start getting visions. She came, she really did. Couldn't she have waited a second? No, not for a second, otherwise I'm going to start sounding like Signora Sanfelice: "Just a sec." It was Anna, behind the window once again. I didn't even smell her scent. I didn't even hear her voice: I recognized the word Sunday from the movement of her mouth. The look on my face must have been idiotic.

I went to the mirror to see the face that had seen Anna. Eyes popping, hangdog mouth, uneven jaw: the portrait of an idiot, confirmed. I looked like the astonished shepherd in the Christmas crèche.

Don Gaetano came back.

"I'll make you coffee."

"No, I already had some at the widow's." He was refreshed. "You look like your father. You're thin, bony like him, but he was one big twisted nerve, he scattered sparks from his bones. His body acted as a dynamo with the air. You look like him, but a calmer version. It's the same chassis, but with you the engine is improved."

He was answering my thoughts, he heard them all.

. . .

"Don Gaetano, since yesterday when you told me about him I can't settle down. Ever since I was a child I imagined I was a fragment of this building, my father was the building, my mother the courtyard. I used to rummage through every corner, so I would get to know them. It was a version that kept me company and made darkness my friend. Since yesterday I've been going around trying to find whom I should resemble."

Don Gaetano listened while doing the cleaning up, interrupted by the passing by of tenants. We were used to it and picked up where we left off.

"Now I'm no longer a fragment of this building, now that it's gone you can see that it's missing. I'm like everyone else, a child who resembles a couple of people. I don't want to be a son, I want to remain a fragment. If you don't mind, I think I resemble you. Not by heredity, but by imitation, I do the things you teach me and so I get closer."

Don Gaetano passed me the job he was doing. He was connecting the electric wires to a Christmas light, to attach to the outside door.

I sat down to continue. From behind he placed a hand on my shoulder.

"You're a man, you should know how things stand. You don't resemble me, I grew up without parents, but if someone had let me know who they were, I would have searched high and low for them."

From his pocket he pulled out a package, long and narrow, wrapped in newspaper.

"This is for you, open it."

"A gift, Don Gaetano? A gift for me?"

It was the first time a gift had happened to me. I kept holding the wires to the light in my hand.

"Open it."

I put the work down, touched the package, realized what it was. I swallowed without saliva. I unwrapped it and squeezed the bone handle of a knife. Don Gaetano took it and swept the blade over the hairs on his wrist to show me how sharp it was. He folded the blade back into the handle.

He handed it back to me and asked me to open it. The blade came out smooth, effortless.

"You have to carry it, it has to stay with you. It has to be a pair of underwear, without it you're naked. Close it now and stick it in your pocket, tenants are coming."

"This is an important gift, I have to repay you."

"You will repay someone, not me. When the time comes, you will give a knife to a young man and you will have paid your debt. I got my first from a sailor who left it on the ground after a brawl. I picked it up, gave it back to him, he left it to me."

. . .

In the city everyone had a knife in his pocket. I knew but I had never wanted to have one myself. Now that it was in my pocket, it obviously had to stay. Because I was a city kid, not because I was a man. The passage from boy to what came after was something other people knew. For me I was the same as before, twisted in thought, an apprentice of everything.

"You won't use it to slice bread, to clean your nails. You'll use it to defend yourself. When you find yourself against the wall, unable to take a step back even if there is room, then you'll grip it, holding it like this, low, right between your legs."

He showed me the position.

"And you'll look in the eyes of the adversary who's come to block your way. You won't take your eyes off his pupils."

Don Gaetano realized I was staring him in the face.

"It won't happen, but that's what it's used for, only that. It's life insurance."

I nodded yes with my head and went back to the wires.

. . .

The old man from a *basso* at the top of the alley dropped by. He knocked on the glass, Don Gaetano let him in. He was dressed shabbily, a patched-up jacket and a faded beret. He removed it out of respect, told Don Gaetano that his wife had been in bed for three days.

"*Nun pozzo e chiamma' 'o miedico, nun ce stanno denari—* I can't call the doctor, we haven't got the money. *Putesse veni' 'stu giuvinotto vuost' che è studiuso 'e libri?—* Could your boy come, since he has book learning?"

Don Gaetano looked at me.

"I study Latin, not medicine."

"*Sempe studiuso siete e ne sapite cchiù 'e nuie ca simmo senza scuola*"—You're still a student, you know more than us, we never went to school.

There was no way out, I went with the man, who thanked me over and over again.

I went into their home, into the stench of misery, acrid and smoky. On a bench three women were mumbling the rosary. The old woman was laid out on a cot, moving her lips mechanically, eyes closed. I touched her forehead, a fever. I lifted her bedsheet, there was a stench of sores, the beginning of ulcers around her heels.

"Bedsores," I said softly.

Behind me one of the three asked what I'd said.

"*La paga di subbito*"—Better pay up.

"*Oh mamma mia,*" said one of them in reply.

"*Giuvino', vi pavammo oggi a otto*"—Young man, we'll pay you eight days from today.

"What do you think he is, a *pizzaiolo*, that you pay eight days from today?"

I told the old man we needed bandages and ointment. I went to the pharmacy. I was happy to have some money in my pocket. I bought what was needed, recommended by the pharmacist, including pills for the fever. I went back and treated the sores, which were just beginning. The pill was tough, she'd never swallowed one before. I went to the baker, he gave me a slice of bread, I made a little ball out of the soft part with the pill inside, and in this way she took it.

The rosary continued, pleased it had produced an intervention. The old man wanted to kiss my hands, we had a tug of war. I told him to keep giving her the pills and left.

. . .

Don Gaetano was settling a fight between two tenants. One complained that her upstairs neighbor was hanging out her laundry so it would drip on top of hers, which was almost dry. It was a simple enough matter, but they had to scream about it so the whole building would know. Don Gaetano listened to the two squalling throats, ready to tear each other's hair out.

They had started from the balconies and he had invited them to bring it down to the loge. As I got there they were going at it, already hoarse. I sat back down at the table to connect the wires. There were often paste-ups because there were so many of us, one on top of the other. They happened because of friction. They're called paste-ups because they have a sticky adhesive that slimes the words and pushes them toward the hands, and then it takes a solvent to divide them. Don Gaetano used to say, "The donkeys quarrel and the wagon breaks." For quarrels between women he offered a magic potion: a cup of coffee.

They made up with each other. Don Gaetano's coffee had legal powers, it was the Supreme Court. It settled disputes. To add my own two cents to the success, I turned on the Christmas lights. They hugged and left arm in arm, telling each other their secrets.

"Don Gaetano, what do you put in the coffee to get this effect?"

"*'A pacienza*, I put in some patience. It's a root that grows in our alleys. They needed to let off some steam, to get out of the house, find someone to listen to them."

. . .

The days of the week passed by, December had arrived. The volcano wore snow on its summit, at night the north wind made ice on the ground and crystal in the sky.

"*Pare 'nu cummoglio di preta turchese*"—It looks like a blanket of turquoise: the second-floor tenant, Professor Cotico, a retiree, had dedicated himself to poetry. He would compose, then he would drop by the loge to recite the verses he had just written. The north wind inspired him.

"*Friddo 'a matina, che spaccava ll'ogne*"—So cold in the morning it split your nails.

"*Prufesso'*, this has already been written and set to music, the verses are by Ernesto Murolo."

"Really? No sooner does a guy finish writing a verse, then out pops someone who says, 'I was there first.' But gentlemen, poetry is not a streetcar where the first to arrive gets a seat and all the others have to stand. Poetry is not a foot race where you have to come in first. Every day is born innocent to poetry, a person wakes up and renews it."

"Yes, of course, the early bird rewrites *The Divine Comedy*."

"Don Gaetano, you are too harsh a judge. Listen to this other verse:

> *e pure a mezzogiorno*
> *'o friddo s'accaniva senza scuorno*

> even at midday
> the cold persevered unabashed.

"That one is all yours, *prufesso'*, no one can take it from you, you can put your copyright on it."

"Well it was about time!"

. . .

That autumn I got to know the tenants. From the loge you could see them passing one at a time, so they stood out from each other. The loge window was a magnifying glass for stamp collectors. They were less interesting than the characters I read about in Don Raimondo's books, but more specialized. Each of them had given himself a persona to stand out from the others and not disappear into the mass of people we were. Faces competed to differ from each other as much as possible, and so did all the voices and hellos and habits. They responded to a law: thou art unequal, distinguish thyself from one another. They applied it scrupulously. One person had a canary (*canarino*) on the balcony, the next-door neighbor put out a gold-finch (*cardellino*), so the downstairs neighbor got a cross between the two called the canary-goldfinch (*'o 'ncardellato*). A well-to-do woman had three medium-sized dogs and she took them on walks with three long leashes that twisted around every obstacle in the alley. The old man from the basso, the one who had come about his sick wife, used to place his chair in front of the door to have a smoke. Every time without fail the dogs would surround him with their leashes and end up moored to his chair, shifting it and making it tot-ter. After untangling the leashes, in the wake of the woman roaring on in her descent, you could hear the comments of neighbors across the way: "The signora is out hunting once again."

. . .

Cummoglio, the accountant, is an unlucky business-man. He comes from a family of button manufac-turers, *buttunari*, ruined by the dawn of the zipper. Before the war he had started selling wooden ice-boxes, but had to close because of competition from the refrigerator. Patiently he shifted into the wool mattress business just when spring mattresses were making their debut.

Don Gaetano used to say if he threw a stalk of straw into the water it would sink to the bottom, while others could even get lead to float. His wife, Euterpe, had given birth to twins, my age, named Oreste and Piliade, like the inseparable friends of Greek mythology. They were so alike not even their parents could tell them apart. They deliberately confounded people, the same haircut, same knot of the tie; if one got a cut the other wore a Band-Aid, too. They burst into laughter at the same time. They applied themselves scrupulously to their alikeness. They took advantage of it, trading places and names. They themselves must have believed they were one and the other at the same time. They had put their efforts into being double.

Signor Cummoglio had given up on telling them apart and he didn't call them by name. He had given them a collective nickname, *I Vuie*, You-Two. To that they would gladly answer. If he wanted to call one of them, he would say, "One of You-Two." Even in the building we called them "the You-Twos."

That school year I noticed one difference between them. One of the two could not pronounce the slurred Neapolitan *sh*, as in *shcuola*, *shchifo*, *shfizio.**

He needed to separate them, he'd say *sh-cuola*. The *sh* gave him trouble, just a bit. The other pretended to have the same problem, to cover up.

But sometimes he would forget, that's when I noticed. I had decided that Piliade was the one who could pronounce the *sh* while Oreste couldn't: *'O rest'* in Neapolitan means the remainder. Oreste was missing a small remainder of sameness.

In class that autumn I started calling them by their names without confusing them. They were shocked that they might lose their twoness. They asked me in private how I was able to tell them apart. I said I wouldn't tell anyone how, not even them. "You can keep the secret of your name, I'll keep the one of how I know."

It worked.

I was very reserved, secrets and hiding places were safe with me.

---

* Neapolitans tend to pronounce the initial *s* in Italian as *sh*, hence *scuola* (school) becomes *shcuola*, *schifo* (disgust) becomes *shchifo*, and *sfizio* (whim) becomes *shfizio*.

"We believe you," one of the two said. They used the pronoun "we" naturally. I had no opportunity to say it and I liked hearing theirs.

From that moment on I was a danger to them. They avoided me, if I addressed them by name neither of the two replied.

. . .

Sunday arrived unattended. And it passed. Anna didn't come. I spent the afternoon at the loge finishing up a second Christmas light to place over our window. Don Gaetano went out for a walk. The courtyard was filled with glittering light, polished by the chill of the north wind.

The sun beat against the window glass of the top floors and spattered in rebounds down to the ground. The windows of Naples traded the sun with each other. Those that had more because of their position passed it down to those that had less. They were synchronized. The master glaziers mounted them at a slant deliberately, to increase the reflecting surfaces. Down at the loge, a pile of light arrived that did ten laps before ending up in the hole where I lived. Don Gaetano says it's a good sign. The sun is fond of those who live on the lower floors where it doesn't arrive. More than anyone else it loves the blind, to whose eye sockets it gives a special caress. The sun doesn't like the worshippers who lie out naked under its abundance and use it as a colorant for their skin. It wants to warm the coatless, whose teeth chatter in the narrow alleyways. He calls them outside, makes them leave their cold rooms and rubs them until they smile from the tickling. "It's a good sign, the sun is fond of you and is sending its regards inside your little room. The windows are its stairway, the light descends them out of affection for you. It's a sign the sun is protecting you."

. . .

I didn't wait for Anna outside. If she knocked on the main door I would hear her. I played with the knife. It had a white bone handle, I grazed my cheek with the blade to test its sharpness. I remembered Don Gaetano's advice, to keep it for protection, nothing else. You shouldn't get too familiar with a knife, it was a serious tool. Treat it with respect and it will do its duty when the need arises. Play around with it instead, show it off, and it will slip from your hand at the wrong time.

The knife and men of the South go together.

I didn't let myself imagine how I would use it in a dangerous spot. I would improvise. A violent move shouldn't be premeditated. A violent move was throwing yourself between feet to grab the ball with your hands. Violence wasn't the kick in the nose but the dive between feet. If I thought about it first I wouldn't do it. So it must go with the knife. In the event of danger, I will find the defensive maneuver.

. . .

Don Gaetano came back and we started hanging the lights. On the outside door and on the loge window the blinking lights winked at the holiday. With this Don Gaetano freed himself of the obligation to celebrate the recurrence. He didn't put up the crèche.

"The crèche is for persons with children and are teaching them to love the holy story."

We did not have nor were we a family.

Those who had a social position used Christmas to flaunt it. At the loge baskets arrived for them filled with an abundance of things to eat, a feast for the eyes. Those who had nothing dug themselves into debt so they, too, could show off. La Capa took his family to the theater in a taxi. Then he dropped by to talk about it. His wife, a tub, went out in a party dress, but she was still a tub wrapped in a curtain with a lampshade on top. She called the taxi driver *scioffè*—chauffeur. La

Capa was both mortified and proud, so he kept Don Gaetano informed.

"The other night at the San Carlo opera they were performing *'o Fallesta'*."

"*Falle sta' come*—Make him stay what? Make him stay quiet?"

"Don Gaeta', the opera *'o Fallesta'*."

"What do you mean *Falle sta'*? Make him stay good?"

"*Gnernò*, it's just plain *Fallesta'*.

"Why? Didn't he want to stay?"

Don Gaetano was scared of La Capa but he didn't let him get away with anything. La Capa couldn't manage to say *Falstaff*.

"Don Gaetano, I can't believe with all your schooling, you don't know the operas of maestro Ver—, Ver—, what's the guy's name?"

"*Verme*"—Worm?

"*Nun me saccio arricurda' 'o nome 'e stu maestro*—I can't remember the maestro's name, *Ver, Ver* . . ."

"*Verza*"—Cabbage?

"*Gnernò, nun era verza*—No, it wasn't cabbage. To make a long story short, all the best society was there, *'o prefetto, 'o quistore, 'o sinnaco*—the prefect, the police chief, the mayor—*con tutt'a giubba comunale*—with the whole town gowncil."

"Ah, he wanted to put it on."

"Put what on?"

"'*A giubba*"—The gown.

"What gown? Don Gaetano, you're getting me confused with these details."

With La Capa you could never finish a story, he gave up.

The latest was that his wife had got him to buy her a *barboncino* (poodle). "*Perché fa scicco*"—because it's "sheik"—she had told her husband. They had taken a white one home. La Capa had a consultation with Don Gaetano.

"What do you say, Don Gaetano, are we doing the right thing to get this Bourbon dog?"

"You have to call it Ferdinand."

"Do you think?"

"Of course, the Bourbons have to be called Ferdinand. If it's a Savoia it has to be called Umberto."

"No, it's a Bourbon, through and through."

I asked Don Gaetano why a serious and hardworking man like La Capa allowed himself to be made a fool of, and willingly. A man who had known the gravity of misery, now he had a few conveniences and ruined himself by his obsession with passing for a gentleman.

"For a poor guy with money the first thing is to buy himself a suit. He puts on an expensive fabric and thinks he's another person. But that's all money can do, make you seem. La Capa wants to seem and that's why he stumbles. When he was bent over to get a shoe size no one laughed. They say money doesn't stink, but it does stink and it makes the people who wear it stink, too."

At the beginning of the month come the visits of Signorina Scafarèa, promptly behind in her rent payment. Every day she makes an appearance: "Has the money order arrived?" She is waiting for the remittance from her brother in America. She gets by on that money. With one half she pays the rent and with the other she struggles for a month. She's as dry as a prune, a garlic breath that could make flies drop. When she finds our window open she never fails to pop her head in with a question, leaving her signature on the air.

She drops by at lunchtime, she can ruin your appetite. When the money order arrives Don Gaetano rushes to bring it to her.

. . .

I see Anna again outside the school. She's sitting at the cafe across from the gate with her bottle-blond friend. It was a day for lizards to crawl out from under the rocks to console themselves in the sun. After the pounding of the north wind the sirocco was a caress. The cafes had set up the tables outdoors.

She waved and signaled for me to come over. I was ashamed to stand in front of the two of them like a schoolboy with books under my arm.

"I think I will take the apartment. One day soon I'll come by to take the measurements, can you give me a hand?"

"At your service." I remained stiff and nothing more came out of me. The other girl mimicked my "at your service" and laughed. She was right, was that any way for me to reply? I wasn't even expecting Anna, never mind her being so formal with me. I took my leave, embarrassed. As if she'd said "thee," I thought. A smile at my own expense broke out. There are days devoted to being ridiculous, even without La Capa's money. Facing the two of them at the cafe I couldn't put on the veneer of seriousness I had at the loge. Maybe I was ridiculous there, too, without realizing it.

The meeting had not happened by chance. It must have been Anna who found me, chose the place, and feigned surprise. Did she mean to reassure me that she would come back? I asked deep within myself and heard Anna's thoughts answering: yes. I ran smack into a man who was standing there.

"Mind your manners, young man."

"Excuse me, I'm sorry, I didn't see you."

"Yeah, right, so now I've become invisible?"

Anna's laughter came to me from inside.

Why did she have to pretend? Was she being spied on, was the other girl checking up on her? No answer came.

Was I also receiving thoughts, like Don Gaetano? Anna's had come to me and mine had gone to her. I tried again, nothing, the line had dropped.

Sometimes a move succeeds and you don't know how. Try it again, it doesn't come.

Things happen to me by mistake. I tried to reconstruct the circumstances: what had I been like the day before happiness? How had I been five minutes before when I was asking Anna for confirmation and I smacked into someone? I had already forgotten and I couldn't redo it.

I got to the loge to find Don Gaetano already at the table.

"Don Gaetano, I brought you the baccalà already spongy, the way you like it."

"You shouldn't have gone to the trouble, anyone could smell from the door that you were bringing baccalà. Come in and have a seat."

"And anyone can smell from the door you're cooking pasta with potatoes, what a treat."

I washed my hands, which were seasoned with baccalà, and from the bathroom I said I had seen Anna.

"She says she wants to come live here."

"She's lying."

"So what do you think Anna wants?"

Don Gaetano let me sit down and start to chew on the first few spoonfuls.

"Anna wants to see blood."

I couldn't wait and asked with my mouth still full.

"And what's she going to do once she's seen it?"

Don Gaetano cleaned his mouth, drank a sip of wine.

"Blood is truth. It doesn't lie when it goes out and it doesn't come back. That's the way words should be, after you say them you can't take them back. Anna wants to see the truth bleed out."

He spoke softly. He was saying something simple, I didn't understand it. I preferred to keep my mouth closed around the pasta and potatoes. You could see that happiness was a truth and that its price was blood.

"Anna will come back," I said, to indicate there was nothing I could do about it.

Don Gaetano nodded yes with his head. I wiped my bowl clean.

"She was pretty outside the school. She was wearing nylon stockings, shaking her hair in the sunlight. She's interested in me, the most ordinary guy in town, a guy who doesn't count for anything."

"Don't put yourself down before anyone. You're good stuff and you'll show them." Don Gaetano had my back. "A guy who grew up alone inside a little room and behaves well by instinct has a special life. You have to defend it, even through trial by blood."

. . .

What he said didn't surprise me. Before Anna I used to think blood belonged in the body circulating in the dark. It had nothing to gain from coming out and drying in the light. Outside the body it was useless. Now I knew that it was useful to Anna, maybe she would be healed to see blood let out in front of her. I knew I was ready, it didn't matter when. "Yes": Anna's voice reached me again. Then yes, I promise I will obey the yeses, I will say yes more than no, in my life my moves will be ruled by a majority of yeses. The no, even if I have to say it, will be subservient to the yeses. Will I spare my blood before Anna? No.

"Her boyfriend, the gangster, has been released from prison. At Christmastime they let them out."

"I knew she had a boyfriend. I'm happy for Anna he's free."

Don Gaetano started clearing, I washed the dishes.

"Someone has to go up to the widow's, do you want to go?"

"Did she ask you to send me?"

"Don't ask questions when women are involved. Do you want to go?"

A warmth descended from my stomach downward. "OK."

. . .

The months of sweaty embraces had passed. Anna, who had wanted me, had passed. She has sucked the stone and spit it out. I looked for the changes in the mirror. My face was the same: long, easily bewildered, with blurry eyes. My nose was more swollen, a gloomy purple still on my cheekbones. My body was sharper, there was more emphasis to the ribs, the curves of my chest, and small rounded muscles were moving over my stomach. By her there was warmth, she opened in a dressing gown, took my hand, and I followed her into the bedroom. Haste came over me and I force-fully embraced her. Rather than the bed I pushed her against the wall and without getting undressed we did the thrusts standing. Rather than let her do the moves, I did my own, improvised. I was taller, she grabbed hold of me, lifting first one leg, then the other. I found her in my arms, her feet behind my back. I held her this way until I emptied myself, finished. I carried her away from the wall and laid her on the bed. She smoothed my sweaty hair, kissed me all over my face. Then she made coffee and wanted to bring it to me in bed. Such attentions from her were new. I saw a smile I had never seen when she entered with the tray. Our embraces were silent, her smile replaced the missing words. I drank the coffee of a gratified man. She accompanied me and lifted the toolbox up to my shoulders.

The door closed after I had arrived at the first landing.

· · ·

Something had happened that made me different to others. The respect of the world arrived in an instant. You don't expect it and can't explain it. Something had happened at the loge, too. The window had been broken. Don Gaetano had called the master glazier, who was taking measurements. I didn't ask, there were strangers. Professor Cotico issued the sentence: "Damage to window and loge, twenty-seven and sixty-eight, good numbers." Don Gaetano left me in charge and went off with the glazier. Tenants dropped by and said hello the same way they did with Don Gaetano. The count came by: "My dear sir, you owe me a rematch, don't forget." He had addressed me formally. I was dumbfounded, a dizziness passed through my body and demanded sleep.

The glazier came back an hour later without Don Gaetano. I helped him to mount the new glass, to attach it with putty. It was a little crooked.

· · ·

Don Gaetano found the work all done and the loge in order. I asked how it had happened.

"You didn't hear anything while you were at the widow's?"

"Nothing."

"Anna's boyfriend dropped by, he was looking for you. He played the tough guy, knocked the table over. He wanted to know where you were. People started staring. He punched his gloved hand through the glass, someone started screaming, *'le guardie*—call the cops, and he left. He said he'd be back and where he finds you, he'll leave you."

"And you, did he do anything to you, did he touch you? Did he insult you?"

My voice was loud, I was surprised at myself, overcome by anger toward the man who had threatened him in my place.

"He didn't do a thing to me, only the bravado of the table and the glass."

This is why people had changed toward me from one minute to the next. The rumor had spread. Don Gaetano asked me what I wanted to do.

"Nothing, this is where Anna will find me, this is where he will find me." The words came out by themselves, they decided for me. Once said, they couldn't be taken back.

When I heard them, I knew they were right. Was this the blood that Anna needed? The blood of two young guys facing off? Was this what Don Gaetano had warned me of? A man realizes things when they hit him over the head. I smiled at Don Gaetano, a smile of appreciation for the knife. He indicated yes with his head, a solemn yes, slightly embarrassed.

"It won't be today," I said. "Let's go on about our business, I'll start cooking potatoes, onions, and tomatoes, then I'll lower the baccalà into it. And we'll play another hand of scopa."

. . .

Don Gaetano let me be. I could see clearly around myself, outside was the early darkness of December. The fresh putty on the new window smelled of wax and rubber. The baccalà smoked fragrantly, thoughts were the clothes on the line. The scopa cards told me the sequence in which to play them. I could guess the ones in Don Gaetano's hand. Or else he was telling me.

"Don Gaetano, can you transmit your thoughts to another person?"

"No, I receive them, that's all there is to it."

"Don Gaetano, tonight you're distracted, I don't know you, you let me take a seven and I'm holding *denari*."

"I was forced. I'm not distracted, you're the one who's playing tonight as if you were in heaven. I don't think I can win."

"The broken glass and the nasty visit have put you out of sorts."

"I'm the same player I am every night, you're the one who's changed and don't realize it."

I didn't realize. I wasn't surprised even to win two hands in a row. I didn't see the difference from the usual times when I lost. I stood up to flip the baccalà over in the pan together with the rest. They knocked on the window. Don Gaetano stood up in a flash and went to the door. Rather than let the person enter he went out. I looked at them from the other side of the window while tasting the cooking. I couldn't see their faces. The gentleman was dressed elegantly, a nice tan overcoat, he made short movements with his hands. Don Gaetano kept his behind his back, leaning slightly forward to listen. The man made a gesture that concluded the conversation. He placed his hand on his wallet, Don Gaetano stopped his arm, the man insisted on giving him money. He was forced to take it, the man pressed it into his hand. It must have been the money for the new glass. The man placed a hand on Don Gaetano's shoulder, they embraced. He came back in and I asked with my eyes what it was. He let the money fall to the table.

"This is worth the life that is played heads or tails, a windowpane reimbursed and the verdict of the neighborhood boss: *Nun pozzo fa' niente*—there's nothing I can do about it—*'o bbrito se pava, l'annore no e se lava'*."

'O bbrito—it had been a long time since I'd heard the name for glass in dialect. Glass you pay for, not honor. Dialect was special for verdicts, better than the Latin mass.

"You asked him to intercede, Don Gaetano? Forget about it, we'll take care of it between ourselves and maybe no one will get hurt. Don't give it a second thought."

He nodded a defeated yes.

. . .

That night we savored a baccalà fit for kings, we drank the wine and Don Gaetano told me the war stories that opened my ears and expanded my heart.

The Germans had mined the aqueduct to blow it up. A group of them were taken prisoner by the Neapolitans, and to save their lives they said they knew the locations of the explosives. Don Gaetano and the other had been ordered to go with the prisoners to defuse the charges.

The Neapolitans had taken guns from the barracks. Sometimes with a little persuasion, the carabinieri had distributed their equipment out of loyalty to the king. At other barracks the fear of German reprisals made them refuse requests for guns. Then the people came back a little more roughly to requisition them. There was a second front, the Fascists shooting down on the rebellious crowd from the houses. There were battles along the staircases of buildings, on the roofs, summary executions. One of our men was captured by the Germans and placed against the wall, but at that moment a German officer arrived, pursued by our guys, so he shielded himself with the body of the man against the wall. This is how the Germans tried to open up an escape route, but everywhere they were surrounded and attacked. Our man, a brave guy, managed to save himself. His name was Schettini, an acquaintance of Don Gaetano.

I listened to the stories of the city and I recognized it as my own. Don Gaetano had delivered to me, in teaspoons, his belonging to the city. It was the story of many who had banded together to become a people. It had been quickly forgotten. It was good like the baccalà in the pan. At moments of greatness we happen to fight in waves of the southwest wind against the barriers, persist for three days and leave an air of cleanliness in the lungs.

.   .   .

"On Via Foria the streetcar barricades held back the Panzer tanks for hours. In the end they managed to get through but not to Via Roma. From the hillside alleys men and boys descended on the attack, throwing bombs and fire between the tracks of the tanks. Against those legions of the possessed, there was nothing the armored tanks could do, they retreated."

I asked him how a revolt starts.

"The first day's assault was against a German truck that had gone to plunder a shoe factory. In the last days of September the Germans started looting what they could from the stores and even from the churches. It started with an improvised attack on one of their trucks filled with shoes, the first battle.

"The American ships were in sight, the Germans about to leave: why take a risk when liberation was so close? In Rome, months later, nothing happened in the same conditions, the people had waited.

"The retreat wasn't a sure thing, the Germans had enough forces to resist. They had prepared defenses against a landing in the city, they were prepared to fight. And their anger was hardened. The men in hiding were pushing to come out of the tufo underground, there was the forced evacuation of the coastal strip, three hundred meters from the sea all houses had to be emptied. The city leans into the sea, to empty it for a width of three hundred meters meant one hundred thousand displaced people from one day to the next, camped out, they didn't know where to go. Yes, we could have waited around all the same, kept our heads down and counted the passing hours. So I don't know why we leaped up like crickets into the streets all at once. The things you throw yourself into doing in those hours belong in part to you, the rest belongs to that body known as the populace. It's everyone around, people doing like you and you doing like them. One minute you are in front of everyone, the next they overtake you, one guy falls dead and in his name the others carry on what he started. It resembles music. Each person plays an instrument and what emerges is not the sum of the players but music, a current that moves in waves, flays the sea, a hunger that shows you the bread on the ground, and you leave it for someone else, a mother who hands a stone to her child, the commotion that brings blood and not tears to the eyes. I don't know how to explain it to you, the revolt. If you find yourself in the middle of one, you'll join in and it won't resemble the one I'm telling you about. But it will be equal, because all revolts of the people against armed forces are sisters."

. . .

I understood the uprising in fits and I imagined it in fits, like the resurrection of a body. At first a nervous contraction, then the muscle of a finger that moves, a tic, a reawakening that starts from the periphery of the body. Only after sitting up did Lazarus remember hearing the voice that ordered him to arise. This is how I pictured the uprising, the discharge of energy in a spent body. But how had it come to extinguish itself, how had it been reduced to a tin soldier?

At school I would never hear a lecture as precise as Don Gaetano's story. At school we studied up to the First World War, and then both the school year and the twentieth century came to an end. A young man shot an archduke and the world waged war on itself, divided between those who took the archduke's side and those who took the young man's. The First World War was one long trench, a place where men stand with their feet in a ditch. But the Second World War, the relapse? I couldn't picture the youths that had been melted into tin soldiers. They had been transformed into the adults around me, the most troubled, decimated generation in the history of the world.

"I knew a young guy, he was twenty years old at the beginning of the war. He was a good person, studious, poor, hardworking. To get by he gave private lessons to students. He fell in love with a girl, went to her house to teach her Italian and math. But we only found out about his falling in love after. He was in deep mourning, his father had died. He wore a black jacket with holes at the elbows, so worn out it was shiny. He fell in love and was sad that he couldn't wear a little color. He was passionate about his subject, he knew many verses of Dante by heart. In June 1940 Italy entered the war and he enlisted as a volunteer. He didn't expect to be called up, didn't take advantage of being his mother's sole support, entered the navy as an ensign. And finally he was able to remove his mourning, happy to be able to present himself in the blue uniform of the navy. His speech was filled with patriotism, but his real enthusiasm was for the colorful uniform he wore. He made his appearance in it to give his last private lessons. The girl, who found out later she was loved, wrote compositions that he saved. His mother, the widow, told her when she went to visit her.

"To make a long story short, no sooner had he embarked than he died in the naval clash off Cape Teulada, in the month of November 1940. He had a nice dark complexion, serious, full of goodwill, and the blue uniform draped him in the clothing of a youth he had never known. That's how it happens that a person is thrown into war, and don't you dare think it's a small thing."

"I wouldn't dare, Don Gaetano, I would do it for Anna."

"At the end of the uprising the first American jeep drove up the seafront, preceded by one of our soldiers in a Bersagliere uniform shouting, '*È fernuta, avimmo vinciuto*'—It's over, we've won. The Germans were still in Capodimonte with heavy artillery to cover their retreat.

"Right away a black market began in American goods coming off the ships. From the depots their abundance disappeared by the truckload. For transportation even the sewers were used."

In the center of Santa Lucia Don Gaetano saw a manhole cover lift up, a head pop out and look around. He went up to offer him a hand getting out, the guy answered, "Sorry, I'm on the wrong street." He popped back down and closed the manhole cover behind him.

That night lasted longer than the others. Don Gaetano was entrusting me with a history. It was an inheritance.

His stories became my memories. I recognized where I came from, I wasn't a child of the building but of the city. I wasn't an orphan but a person in a populace. We took leave of each other at midnight. I stood up from the chair and I had grown, I was taller, beneath my feet was a soil that lifted me up by new inches. He had given me a sense of belonging. I was from Naples, with the compassion, rage, and even the shame of one who is born late.

· · ·

In my room I thought about the other day before, the Saturday with Anna. That other day before was better. It contained a growth, the sudden respect of the persons around, the widow's coffee, the winning hands of scopa. This day before contained more energy. Was I diminishing Anna? No, I was putting her on top of everything. The days before and the days after all depended on her. My yes to everything came from her. I slept smooth and deep. Upon reawakening my first move was for the knife. I thought: it's not for now. Don Gaetano was upstairs doing the cleaning, I left him a note saying hello. In the alley one man greeted me by tipping his hat with his hand.

At school I listened deeply to the lessons. I realized how important the things I was learning were. It was good that a man presented them to an assembly of seated youths, that they had a knack for listening, for grasping at once. Good the classroom where you stay to learn. Good the oxygen that bonds with the blood and carries blood and words to the depths of the body. Good the names of the moons around Jupiter, good the Greeks' cry of "The sea, the sea" at the end of the retreat, good that Xenophon wrote it down so it would not be lost. Good, too, Pliny's account of the eruption of Vesuvius. Their writing absorbed the tragedies, transformed them into narrative material to transmit and therefore outlive them. Light entered the head the way it entered the classroom. Outside it was a bright day, a May day that had landed in the bouquet of December.

· · ·

I headed home still thinking about the lesson. There was a civil generosity in free public school that allowed someone like me to learn. I had grown up inside and I hadn't noticed the effort of a society to put this duty into practice. Education gave importance to us poor people. The rich would get educated anyway. School gave importance to the have-nots, it created equality. It did not abolish poverty, but between its walls it allowed parity. The inequality began outside.

. . .

I dropped by Don Raimondo's to return the book, Neapolitan poetry by Salvatore Di Giacomo, our favorite.

"It's never been more beautiful than this, our language."

"You're right, Don Raimondo, I really liked the descent to the ground of a celestial sheet, which gathers up a crowd of poor people and takes them to eat in heaven. I find some of that taste of manna in Don Gaetano's pasta with potatoes."

Don Raimondo enjoyed exchanging a few words about the borrowed book. That day for the first time I did not ask for one to take away. He was surprised. "I have an exam. I'll go back to reading after." I didn't know whether I would be able to return it.

I was walking light-footed, on my way home from school, which was located in a wide stretch of the road near the sea. At the head of the alley I was met by the

old man whose home I had visited to practice medicine without a license. He grabbed my hand, I shook
it, just in case he started up again with the gotta-kiss-it
gratitude.

"*Nun ce iate, chillo ve sta aspettanno*"—Don't go, that
guy is waiting for you. He stopped me, tried to block
my way. Although there was no wall behind me, there
was no turning back. I had to go to where I belonged.
I asked about his wife, he let go of my hand to remove
his hat and express thanks: "She's fine, thanks to your
good work." I took advantage of his answer to free myself and continue on. His words followed behind me:
"*Nun ce iate, p'ammore 'e Giesucristo, nun ce iate*"—Don't
go, for the love of Christ, don't go.

· · ·

No one else greeted me in my climb up the alley. I
entered through the main door. Anna, I immediately
saw Anna by the window of the loge.

"I'm waiting for you," the voice from the courtyard
wanted to sound tough.

"Not me," I answered to myself more than to him.
"I don't have to wait."

I kept my eyes on Anna as the footsteps came closer.
I smiled at her shiny sugared-chestnut hair.

"I'm waiting for you," the voice from the courtyard repeated even louder. There was no one except the three of us, you couldn't hear a sound, the loge was dark. I placed the books on the ground in front of the door. Anna looked at me, eyes wide, her mouth slightly open. If she was crazy, that was the tense nerve of her beauty.

"Here I am, Anna," I said, and passed in front of her.

I liked the emptiness surrounding us, no distractions, us and only us.

"*Allora piezz'e mmerda, vuo' veni', o t'aggia veni' a prendere pe' 'e rrecchie*"—You piece of shit, are you coming here or do I have come out and grab you by the ears?

I thought he must want the whole building to hear him, not me. Outside school the boys showed off the threats they had learned in the streets, they would say I'm gonna do this to you, I'm gonna do that. I didn't like the repertoire of tough talk with exclamation points. With my head low I entered the courtyard.

In the middle was that voice, but I still hadn't lifted my eyes.

First I looked at the shoes, new, shiny, La Capa would have appreciated them, then the pressed trousers, then the rest: he was in his Sunday best, with a double-breasted jacket, tie, even a boutonniere:

good-looking guy. Black mustache, brilliantine in his hair, Anna had picked a fancy man. He kept his eyes narrowed. For a moment I looked up toward this May sky at Christmastime, then I stared him straight in the face and didn't take my eyes off him.

In his hand he had a knife he was using to pick at his fingernails, I took a few steps forward and realized I was taller. The sun didn't make it to the ground, it ricocheted between the windows and bounced the light back and forth. It occurred to me that the sun was protecting me, as Don Gaetano had said.

I didn't notice that Anna had come into the courtyard behind me. While I drew my knife out of my jacket, a thought came to me and I held on to it tight.

· · ·

"*Si' muorto, piezz'e mmerda*"—You're dead, you piece of shit, he said, and came near. I held the knife low, between my legs, in front of my crotch, the tip pointing to the ground. He gripped on the right, I on the left.

He made a short lunge, then a longer one, I took a step to the side and one to the back. I made no moves to strike, I had to defend myself, the attack was up to him. I noticed Anna because among us was a third breath deeper than ours. With each lunge he made I shifted to the side clockwise. I wanted to circle the courtyard. He lost his patience and came straight at me, shouting, the knives touched, wounding my right arm and grazing his ribs. There went his coat, our first blood ruined his, got the vest dirty, too. It tore my light gray sleeve, a dark blotch, as I saw later. Anna let out a hoarse cry. He looked at his jacket, I took advantage to shift to a spot in the courtyard. A woman's voice shouted, "Stop them, they'll kill each other." There was a noise of windows opening, the blood had broken our solitude observed.

At the sight of the ruined suit he was infuriated by the insult and charged at me sideways, shouting, "*Mo' si' mmuorto*"—You're a dead man! With arms wide he came at me for the mano a mano, I made the move to pull up to my full height, he raised his head to look me in the face and took unshielded the rebound of light I was looking for. He was blinded by the reflection for the amount of time my arm needed, I made my only lunge with the knife, it sank into his side, close to his liver. He collapsed in an instant, threw away the weapon, placed his hands on his side, crumpled to his knees. Anna sputtered sobs and started to cry. I laid the knife on the ground, it had done its job. Standing between us Anna was crying, her face contorted in grimaces of pain. In the light of the courtyard I realized she was covered with bruises.

People were coming, Don Gaetano took me by an arm and led me. In front of the loge I gathered the books. My right arm was bleeding heavily. We cut through the people who were parting before us. Half the building was there. Some said, "He did the right thing," and others cried murderer. The You-Twos were also there, I heard someone say, "*Sh-cansiamoci*"— we'd better get out of here—it had to be Oreste.

My arm hooked into Don Gaetano's, no one stood in the way to stop me. In front of the entry I recognized the tan coat of the night before. I allowed myself to be led. My blood was dropping and so was I. Don Gaetano placed his coat over my arm to cover the wound. Going down the alley we crossed the path of two policemen who were on their way up. We entered a pharmacy. The doctor took us into the back, stopped the blood, and sewed up the cut with a good stitch. They didn't say a word to each other or to me. We left with the purchase of more bandages.

. . .

With Don Gaetano next to me I went down to the seashore. The day was an embrace of nature around the city. In Santa Lucia tourists and hansom drivers had their sleeves rolled up. We walked, I didn't ask. The sun was absorbent, it dried the blood, the paint on the boats, the poverty of those descending from the cold alleyways to benefit from its warmth. For them it felt better on the sidewalk than at home in bed, they begged for charity with smiles of gratitude for the warmth.

Carriages were taking American soldiers on rides. They were the sons of the ones who had arrived after the city was liberated. Why were they still here? Because they were the heirs of that victory. Do you inherit a victory? It should last for as long as the enemy is on the ground, then stop.

It wasn't a victory for me, either, I had only saved myself with the knife. Now I was leaving. There are those who stay, instead, like the Americans. Where was Don Gaetano taking me? Definitely not to the police, maybe it was my turn to live in a hiding place. The one under the loge was no good, Anna knew about it.

I had a feverish exhaustion at the sight of the overwhelming beauty.

"This is where I belong, Don Gaetano."

"Say good-bye to it, tonight you're taking a boat to America. You have a ticket under another name on a ship bound for Argentina. After I'll give you the papers."

"You already knew." What was life made of if you could predict the smallest details? Just to predict it, without being able to intervene, to prevent. This was the calloused sadness of Don Gaetano. He could only compensate with a secondary salvation, a ticket for America, his same voyage. The ocean was an escape route for us of the South. It granted absolution, impossible on earth. My thoughts were making a racket in my head, Don Gaetano was listening to them.

"For us the sea evens the score."

The question came to me, "Are you coming, too?"

"No, I'm staying, I'll watch your back. I'll let you know when you can return. You're going to stay with a friend, he'll come to get you when you land."

Return? I don't think I'll return to the place of the spilled blood. I won't climb back up the slope of the alleyways.

"If I had a father, he wouldn't do this for me."

"We don't know, you and I don't have one, we know nothing about them."

We sat down on a bench facing the sea.

"You're weak, you've lost blood."

"I had extra, I had some for her, too. Its purpose was to make her tears come out. They're precious, Don Gaetano, Anna's tears, they're the escape from her madness. It wasn't our blood she was seeking, but her own tears. She didn't know how to cry. Tears are worth more than blood. How is it you weren't at the loge?"

"I was. I couldn't interfere, we were all there, even the boss from last night. Questions of honor and bravery have to be settled alone, no one can get in the middle. You did good to leave the knife there."

"You are the one who taught me to respect the knife, that its purpose was protection and nothing more. So you were there watching?"

"Yes, and the first blood wasn't enough. The young man had decided that no one could intervene until the last blood. I knew you wouldn't die, but I didn't know how. When I saw you moving in a circle in the courtyard, I realized what you had in mind. You were looking for the heat in the face, the flash point. I could never have imagined you'd be so expert."

"It was the sun in the eyes that had just entered the courtyard. I thought I could bring him to that point. I also knew I wasn't going to die, Don Gaetano. It was one of your thoughts, I listened to it in my head. I'm starting to receive thoughts, too."

"I know. Yesterday you won at scopa. Your days of learning from me are over."

. . .

The ships of the American Sixth Fleet, the aircraft carrier and its convoy, were leaving the gulf in formation. The light gray of their paint dissolved in the high seas. It was the color of my threadbare jacket. My light gray was going off to sea as well. I would have time to mend the cut in the sleeve and wash away the blood.

"Let me know about Anna, she's cured."

We didn't say a word about the fallen youth. Where the knife entered there was no hope.

"Who knows where they're going?" I said, in the direction of the warships.

"Not home, and you neither. You'll go in that direction." He pointed to the south and the west. I looked at the books and the notebooks on my knees, good-bye to school, all the lessons were over at once. The city that had taught me, I was losing, Anna, Don Gaetano, the books of Don Raimondo. "*T'aggia 'mpara' e t'aggia perdere*"—I have to teach you and then I have to lose you, the city was pushing me out to sea. I couldn't continue the life that had raised me, ready as a calzone in the frying oil. It had flipped me over and over, dusted me with flour, and then thrown me into the black skillet. In one of his poems Salvatore Di Giacomo wishes he could be a little fish captured by the lovely hands of Donna Amalia, who will dust him with flour and *'o mena int'a tiella*—throw him into the pan. It was happening to me. Donna Amalia was the city and the black skillet was the ocean.

"Don Gaetano, exhaustion is making me think stupid things."

. . .

We ate at a tavern by the harbor. He gave me the ticket, the documents, the money, his savings.

"I'll pay you back. It won't be like with the knife, that I'll have to repay with another one. This money I'm going to bring back to you."

At random I said the right things. How did I know what I would find in Argentina? What I would do to survive there? Don Gaetano also gave me a deck of Neapolitan cards and a Spanish grammar. We went to take my pictures for the document. Don Gaetano dropped by a print shop to forge the embossed stamp. I boarded the ship at sunset.

I saw the bay switch on the lights from Posillipo to Sorrento. There were so many white handkerchiefs, waving good-bye to the open eyes of the departing. The persons nearest to me were dripping with tears. Those nearest to me are not in first class, they have no return ticket.

. . .

Now I am writing pages on the lined notebook while the ship steers toward the other end of the world. Around us the ocean moves or stays still. They say that tonight we will pass the equator.

about the author

Erri De Luca was born in Naples in 1950 and today lives in the countryside near Rome. He is the author of several novels, including *God's Mountain*, *Three Horses* (Other Press), and *Me, You* (Other Press; originally published as *Sea of Memory*). He taught himself Hebrew and has translated several books of the Old Testament into Italian. He is one of the most widely read Italian authors alive today.

about the translator

Michael F. Moore has also translated *Three Horses* and *God's Mountain* by Erri De Luca, and is completing *Not Now, Not Here* by the same author. His most recent translations include *Quiet Chaos* by Sandro Veronesi and *Pushing Past the Night* by Mario Calabresi. He is currently working on a new translation of the nineteenth-century classic *The Bethrothed*, by Alessandro Manzoni.